The
Invisible Worm

The Invisible Worm

by

JENNIFER JOHNSTON

SINCLAIR-STEVENSON

First published in Great Britain by
Sinclair-Stevenson Limited
7/8 Kendrick Mews
London SW7 3HG, England

Reprinted 1991

British Library Cataloguing in Publication Data

A CIP catalogue record for this book is available from the British Library.

ISBN 1 85619 041 2

Photoset by Rowland Phototypesetting Limited
Bury St Edmunds, Suffolk
Printed and bound in Great Britain by
Biddles Limited, Guildford and King's Lynn

For MICHAEL
with aeons of love.

O rose, thou art sick!
The invisible worm
That flies in the night,
In the howling storm,

Has found out thy bed
Of crimson joy,
And his dark secret love
Doth thy life destroy.

William Blake
Songs of Experience

I STAND BY the window and watch the woman running.

Is it Laura?

I wonder that, as I watch her flickering like blown leaves through the trees.

I am Laura.

Sometimes I run so fast that my legs buckle under me; ungainly, painful.

This woman runs with dignity.

I have to say that for her.

Sometimes it is dark and I find it difficult to see her as she passes below the trees, running.

Her clothes are dark colours, the colours of weariness.

It is hard to tell from where or what she is running.

Perhaps, I think to myself, she is running towards something.

I think that on good days.

On the other days I know she is running away.

That makes me laugh.

What's the point in that?

I ask the question aloud and the words spring back at me from the four walls of the room.

She always wears dark clothes.

Sometime, someone must have said to her . . . Black suits you, Laura.

No, I am Laura.

I must remember that, but I seem to remember a voice saying that . . . Black suits you, Laura. Maurice, perhaps.

I do wear black from time to time.

I also like bright colours, pinks and yellows, flame colours and purple. I have always thought purple to be a noble colour, a colour worn by courageous people, by people longing to be noticed.

The running woman never wears purple.

If she were to wear brighter colours it would be easier for me to see her; perhaps it would be of some comfort to me, if I could see her more easily.

Perhaps not.

Perhaps, perhaps not.

I don't suppose it matters much.

'Laura!'

When she passes into the darkness of my unseeing, I still stare out through the panes at the fields, and beyond these fields there are more fields; sand-coloured fields at this time of the year, with patches of grass growing up through the dead winter stubble. Beyond the fields are the hills, and then the sea.

Sand, stones, waves, shells, birds, pebbles, ripples, waves breathing, waves heaving, rolling, spume, spray, pools, wrack, weed, glitter, tiny torn claws, glitter . . . diamonds, pearls. . . .

All this I see through these panes of glass with my x-ray eyes.

'Laura!'

I love lists.

I spend a lot of time making lists; lists of the things I love; lists also of the things I hate. Sometimes I write them down on coloured pieces of paper, but most times I say them inside my head.

Incantations.

'What is this?'

Maurice said it to me once, handing me a yellow rag of paper. I took it from him and held it between my thumb and forefinger.

Tree, branch, twig, bark, leaf, sap, bud, flower, wood, ivy, trunk, smooth trunk, knots, corus-cations, axe, cracking, splitting, raging death.

'It's a list.'

'A list of what, for God's sake?'

'A tree list.'

He snatched the paper from me and threw it into the fire.

It was consumed.

'Sometimes I think you're mad.'

I watched the flames consume my tree.

Mad.

'What is mad?' I asked Maurice.

It must have been winter. The fire consumed my tree.

'The way you carry on.'

That's right, it was winter. It was coming up to Christmas time; ivy trailed from the pictures and red ribbons held holly branches above the doors and windows; another tree, laced with silver and glitter, stood in the corner of the room.

Maurice's family always come here for Christmas; old Mrs Quinlan, that's Maurice's mother, Doreen and her husband Bill, Sean and his wife Madge, and Brigid, who isn't married. They bring the children and we all have a very good time.

It's nice to have the house full.

All the rooms full of sound and movement.

This is my house.

It's strange, really; for three generations it has descended through the female line.

I inherited it from my mother and she inherited it from hers.

I did try to have a daughter.

I believe in continuity, the handing down of secrets; I want someone else to hear the whispers, the breaths from the past, as I have always done; someone else to be stirred by the tremors of memory.

Some of the tremors of memory.

I did try. All those seeds were rejected.

'Laura!'

'Yes.'

'Are you ready?'

'Ready?'

'That's what I said.'

'I have my black gloves and my black bag and a scarf to cover my head.'

'You're ready, then.'

'I suppose so.'

Maurice comes across the room towards me and takes my arm. He bends and kisses my cheek. He smells faintly of Eau Sauvage. I bought him that for his birthday.

I continue to look out through the window. The leaves are acid green, uncurling; the wind lifts them and makes them tremble.

'Don't worry,' he says, in his kind voice. 'Everything will be all right.'

'Spring,' I say, for no reason.

He takes my elbow and walks me towards the door.

Such scenes stay with me.

The feel of Maurice's fingers pressing through my coat and my black woollie will stay with me for ever . . . not of course in the front region of my mind, but I will be able to recall, when I need to, the feel of those fingers, the faint smell of Eau Sauvage, the sound of his steps, confident on the polished parquet as we cross the hall.

Such scenes reverberate and conjure up other scenes in the past: my father's soft, white fingers imprinting their marks on my arms, as he shook me and my feet clattered on the floor and a dog barked at nothing, outside in the sunshine. The sound of my own voice screaming, tears suddenly at the soft corners of my brain.

Some memories are so joyful that you could bask forever in them; others you long to shove back, away, back into the darkness out of which they have sprung uninvited.

I try to exorcise that picture of my father and myself in the hall, as we drive in the car towards the church, by calling into my mind happier, more tranquil recollections. Maurice talks, but I don't hear him; his words patter round me like a summer shower.

The streets round the church are lined with cars; the car park is full; women with nothing better to do stand near the church gate waiting to catch a glimpse of something or someone out of the ordinary; a cabinet minister, a bishop, the diminished red-rimmed eyes of the bereaved.

I will not be crying.

It is a huge, ornate church. We walk past the waiting hearse and the watching women. Maurice holds my arm tight; maybe he thinks that I might escape, fly away like a balloon slipping from the fingers of a child; I don't suppose he does, really;

he is not the sort of person to indulge in flights of fancy.

My mother never put her foot inside this church.

I wonder to myself if, had she lived, she would have been with us now, walking beside us with immaculate dignity.

'A vulgarity,' she once said to me. 'Built on the backs and out of the pockets of people who could hardly afford to feed their children. They paid more towards it than your father ever did, or any of his like, because they felt what they gave; those few pounds impinged on their lives.'

My father always hoped that she would turn.

I remember her laughing at him once.

'Divil a bit of it,' she said. 'Haven't you got my house and my land and my beautiful body? What makes you think you should have my soul as well?'

He hated such irony.

She was the only person in my world who didn't jump when he snapped his fingers, who didn't succumb to his enormous charm. Perhaps I shouldn't say that; perhaps she had indeed succumbed, and thereafter had to protect herself from it.

The organ is playing something sonorous and unrecognisable. Our feet clatter on the tiles as we walk to the front of the church.

The tall windows, alive for a moment as the sun comes from behind the clouds, glow into patterned life; heads, hands, haloes, wings are rich with jewel colours, and cast their muted patterns on the tiles and on the congregation; the brightness passes and the church is dark again.

Of course we have to sit in the front.

I do not look to left or right as I follow the little fellow who leads us along the aisle. I don't recognise him, dressed in sober black; black tie, sombre face . . . a professional, I would think. His walk is that of a professional, unobtrusive, almost obsequious, adapted to my pace, consoling in its smoothness.

He turns and inclines his head slightly towards me as we reach the front pew.

I move past him and kneel down.

Our Father which art in Heaven.

The only prayer that trips from my tongue.

Hallowed be Thy name.

A poem.

Thy Kingdom come.

Thy will be done on earth. . . .

Maurice settles to his knees beside me, dipping his head down towards his hands.

. . . as it is in heaven.

Give us this day our daily bread.

My mother's voice is still in my ears.

And forgive us our trespasses. . . .

. . . as we forgive them that . . .

'Laura!'

. . . trespass against us.

I can't.

I cannot forgive.

Forget it, God.

Forget I ever said those words.

No point in speaking lies to You.

'Laura.'

His elbow nudges me.

'Laura.'

I get up from my knees, angry with myself, that even at such a moment I am unable to overcome hatred.

'What?'

'The President's A.D.C. has just arrived.'

Across the aisle from us he is being settled into the front pew with all due obsequiousness.

My flowers are the only ones on the coffin. Maurice must have organised that gesture.

Spring flowers, yellow and green and white; a laugh almost escapes through my lips. Green, white and yellow.

I never intended such a statement, but I'm sure that the President's A.D.C. has made a pleasant mental note; that the ministers and other dignitaries present will commend me in their hearts.

Along the aisle the flowers are heaped, wreaths, crosses, cushions, sprays; a great sheaf of waxlike lilies lies to the right of the coffin.

There is a rustling at the back of the church; the sound of the organ swells.

We stand up.

The ceremony will take its course.

Oration, peroration, homily, sermon, valediction, obsequy, exequy, benediction.

If I got up and spoke the words I have inside me, what a shock they'd get.

The hole that they dig for you won't be deep enough, dear Father.

How petty to think such a thought in the middle of all this formality.

They dance: the words like music punctuate the movements.

With each amen the tempo changes.

They dance to the glory of whatever God may be: advance, retreat, turn, bow.

Candles dance, men dance, boys dance.

They dance in celebration of my father's life.

I feel cold. As if a wind has penetrated the stone walls and is numbing my body; or perhaps the cold is spreading out from me; maybe it will embrace the whole church, the whole town, the whole island: I will infect this race with my hatred.

Maurice is praying, his hands placed together

like some saint in an Italian painting. His eyes are closed. His face still is tinted with brown from his two weeks in January spent in Mustique.

'Will you come, dote?'

'How can I come. Isn't my father dying?'

'There's nothing you can do about that.'

'I must be here.'

'Suit yourself.'

He'd have got a rare shock if I'd said yes; if I'd rushed up to town and bought the bikinis, the silk shirts, the Ambre Solaire.

That would not have been playing the game at all.

Requiem aeternam dona eis Domine, et lux perpetua luceat eis.

'Forgive me,' he had said.

I had to stoop towards him to catch the words, so frail was his voice.

He pulled with his anguished fingers at the sheet that seemed to weigh him down into the bed.

'Laura?'

Exaudi orationem meam ad te omnis caro veniet.

'Will you?'

The nurse read a magazine in a chair by the window.

That was last week, only last week.

The spring sun, weak and all as it was, hurt his eyes, and we had to keep the blinds half drawn.

I put my hand on his; for a moment his fingers were still; then, as I lifted my hand, the restless, tearing and plucking started again.

'Child?'

Agnus Dei qui tollis peccata mundi . . .

'Yes.'

. . . dona eis requiem.

I whispered, Yes.

'That's all, now,' said the nurse, putting her book

on the table and getting up from the basket chair that crackled as she moved, and her starched apron crackled as she came over to the bed.

Agnus Dei qui tollis peccata mundi . . .

'He's tired. Aren't you tired, pet?'

She took his restless hands in hers and bent smiling towards him.

. . . dona eis requiem sempiternam.

'Laura.'

The procession is forming, the dancers moving slowly from the altar down into the aisle. Without much grace the coffin is lifted onto the shoulders of my four cousins, my father's nephews; their feet clatter as they move slowly down the church. Maurice takes my arm and together we walk between the watching people, as we had done on the day of our wedding.

About a month after the funeral, Maurice brought Dominic O'Hara to the house for tea.

The fields were greening at last, no winter dun to be seen, the gold of whin bushes now lighting the slopes of the hills.

Laura was standing by the window when they came into the drawing room.

A book dangled between her fingers.

'Dr Urbino caught the parrot around the neck with a triumphant sigh: *ça y est*. But he released him immediately because the ladder slipped from under his feet and for an instant he was suspended in air and then he realised that he had died without Communion, without time to repent of anything or to say goodbye to anyone, at seven minutes after four on Pentecost Sunday.'

What a way to go, was what she was thinking as

they came into the room; they presumed that she was staring out of the window at the green fields below the house.

She was startled when Maurice spoke her name.

'Oh . . . ah . . . sorry. . . . Hello. . . .'

She put the book down on the table by the window and rubbed her hands on her skirt as if she were wiping some unfriendly substance from them.

'This is Mr O'Hara, dote. . . . I brought him back for a cup of tea.'

She moved across the room towards the men, her hand outstretched.

'How very nice.'

The tall man with her husband smiled and took her hand.

'Dominic,' he said. 'I hope this is O.K.' He held onto her hand.

'Lovely. I'll just. . . .'

'This is my dote, my lovely Laura.'

'Laura,' said the strange man. He still held onto her hand.

She wriggled her fingers.

'. . . run out and. . . .'

He let go.

'. . . put the kettle on.'

She left the room and closed the door behind her.

'Come over to the fire. Sit down. . . . Cigarette?'

Maurice took a packet of cigarettes from his pocket and held it out towards Dominic – who didn't appear to notice. After a moment he took one himself and lit it.

'Beautiful.'

'Hmn? Ha?'

Smoke drifted from his nose.

'This . . . all this . . . and her, too. She is. . . .'

Suddenly embarrassed, he moved across the room to a glass-lidded case in which several medals and miniatures lay on a velvet cloth. He bent down to get a better view.

'What an interesting medal,' he said. 'No . . . no thanks, I don't smoke.'

'Her grandfather.'

'May I?'

Without waiting for Maurice to answer, he opened the lid of the case and took out the medal.

'I've never seen one of these before.' He peered at it closely. 'Indian? Is it Indian?'

'Probably from Inja. I wouldn't know. I . . .'

He closed down the glass lid and came towards the fire.

'I'm sorry,' he said. 'I shouldn't be poking round among your . . .'

'Hers. They're all hers. She's a magpie . . . never throws anything out. Her mother was the same before her. The place is like a bloody museum.'

'Yes. Yes, I can see that. Wonderful.'

The door opened and Laura put her head round it.

'Some people prefer coffee.'

'Tea's fine for me.'

She nodded and disappeared.

The two men were silent for a moment.

'Her family did that sort of thing, you know . . . Inja and all that. Empire building . . . soldiering. You know the sort of thing?'

'There'll never be enough jobs for everyone in this country.'

Dominic picked up a china figure and looked at the marks on the bottom of it.

'People don't care enough.' Carefully he put the figure back again on the mantlepiece.

'Care?'

'I do like that.' He hunkered down beside a small model of an early railway train in a glass case.

'It's all around. The uncaringness of people . . . the government . . . no one really cares . . . do they? Now, this is truly smashing. Don't you think so? I've never seen anything like this before.'

'Oh . . . yes.'

'What's its history? Who made it? It's so perfect. Do you know?'

'Laura will know. It's hers. She knows. . . .'

Laura came into the room with a tray which she put down on a table by the fire.

Dominic got to his feet.

'That . . . ?' he said, gesturing with his hand towards the model.

'Isn't it lovely,' she said. 'I love it so much. My great-grandfather had it made as a toy for my grand-father, but then he couldn't bear to give it to him, so he had that case made for it and kept it for himself. The doors open and shut . . . you can actually take the people in and out. I was never allowed to play with it unless someone was in the room with me. It's just so perfect.'

'Toys,' said Maurice, almost under his breath.

'Let me pour you some tea,' said Laura.

There was silence as she poured the tea and handed the cups to the two men.

'Mr O'Hara teaches at the college.'

'Dominic,' said Dominic quietly.

'What do you teach?' she asked politely.

'I was up there about the extension to the playing fields and he. . . .'

'Classics.'

'Really?'

'. . . seemed at a. . . .'

'Really.'

'. . . loose end, so I asked him home for tea.'

'You don't come across too many classics teachers these days. Do you have many pupils?'

'Not too many . . . well, not too many worth having. The majority of them have no love in their hearts for Virgil or the plays of Aeschylus. They're only doing classics because they have old-fashioned fathers.'

'He's a rugby man. That's your real strength, isn't it, O'Hara?'

'Well. . . .'

'I never liked Latin. . . .'

'*Amo, amas, amat . . .*' said Maurice.

'I couldn't unscramble the grammar.'

'*Caesar adsum jam forte.*'

Dominic O'Hara sipped at his tea and said nothing.

'*Brutus sic in omnibus.*'

'Aeschylus to Ibsen,' she said, aloud but to herself.

Dominic laughed.

'Boyoboyo. . . .'

'I once met a man who taught drama in an American college. Aeschylus to Ibsen in three terms, he said. Imagine that!'

'Boyoboyoboyo!'

'Or maybe it was three years.'

'That would be a mite more reasonable.'

'It was probably three years.'

'Have a piece of cake?' said Maurice.

'Thank you,' said Dominic.

He took a piece of chocolate cake from the offered plate and stared at it for a moment before he took a bite.

'She makes very good cake.'

Maurice put the plate down on the table as he spoke, and took a piece for himself.

'But she never eats it.'

Dominic, whose mouth was full of cake, looked at her and smiled.

'She only picks at her food, don't you, dote? Like a bird.'

She smiled briefly and walked across the room to the window where she had been standing when they came in. She turned her back to them and stared through the panes at the hills. The shadows of the clouds moved over the earth; patterns of light and shade folded and unfolded.

Behind her their voices sounded, the fire cracked, someone placed a teacup on a saucer.

An unfinished man, she thought, as if he were made from unfired clay: hair, skin, lips, lashes, eyes, all the one dun colour like the fields before the greening happened. I bet he burns in the sun, unlike Maurice. Maurice blossoms in the sun, grows like a healthy plant, shines.

'I always wanted to learn Greek,' she said, to no one in particular.

Maurice laughed. 'My wife is crazy. Hark at her.'

'It's never too late,' said Dominic. She turned round towards them. 'I suffer from lethargy. Energetic intentions, but no follow-through.'

'Dote . . .'

'It's never too late . . .' he repeated the words.

Maurice clattered his cup and saucer down onto the table.

'I have to be off. I always make it my business to be down at the mill for the last hour or so of the day . . . just in case any problems arise. Know what I mean? So . . . can I give you a lift or would you prefer to . . . ?'

'No,' said Dominic. 'I prefer not to walk if I can get a lift.'

He came over to her at the window. 'Lovely view.'

She nodded. 'They knew where to build houses in those days.'

He picked her hand up and looked at it, rather as if it were some interesting object that he had seen lying on a table.

Maurice jangled the coins in his trouser pocket.

'Thank you for the tea.' He dropped her hand as he spoke.

'Any time,' she said.

She turned back to the window and listened to their footsteps, listened to Maurice's laugh in the hall, listened to the hall door slam.

Studs.

Cuff links: gold, silver, some with woven initials, some with polished stones, amber, ruby, onyx; two speckled uncut turquoise stones set in rims of gold.

Tiepins, none as flamboyant as the cuff links.

A gold wristwatch with a black face; it had been a present from someone for whom he had done a favour and he had never worn it. He used to wind it every morning and leave it to tick undisturbed on his dressing table.

A wristwatch, plain silver, with large roman figures. This was the one he had worn as long as I could remember.

A fob watch that had belonged to his father and had a thin gold case, smooth as silk to touch.

Two ivory hairbrushes and a hand mirror to match.

An ornate silver manicure set; he had been very vain about his hands.

'You can always tell a gentleman by his hands,' he said once to my mother and myself, holding out his hands to be admired. My mother had merely smiled and said nothing.

All these objects cover the dressing table in front of me; they are, today, all that is left. I think I will distribute them among his nephews. Maurice has his own more contemporary style of decoration. He wears rings, and a gold chain round his neck with a cross dangling from it, carefully hidden during his working hours.

Yesterday I spent most of the day packing his clothes, suits, shirts, woollies, jackets, shoes, even his underwear, into plastic bags, and this morning I sent them off with Maurice, who was going up to Dublin, to the St Vincent de Paul.

I kept back his evening clothes and the morning suit, the top hats, the silk ties, as I didn't think it would be seemly to send them; I thought that whoever unpacked the plastic bags might laugh at the sight of such old-fashioned and almost useless finery. They still hang in the wardrobe behind me, with little mauve moth-deterrents looped round the tops of the coat hangers.

There's feeding for an army of moths there for years to come.

I threw out all his pyjamas and the sheets and blankets that had covered him for the last year. . . . That was some form of superstition on my part and I didn't tell Maurice; he would have laughed at me and then lectured me about extragavance.

The windows are open behind me and a warm breeze pulls gently at the curtains. I know that when I close the windows the smell will return, but in a week or two I will get the painters in and then the room will become healthy.

There were no papers to go through, no letters, business papers, press cuttings; no diaries, nothing to remind him of his past.

When he came to live here with us, or should I

say die here with us, he brought nothing except his clothes and these objects in front of me on the dressing table.

'I will be no bother to anyone,' he said as he came in the front door, leaning on the arm of Nurse Mulcahy. Her shoes squeaked as they walked across the hall.

He held out his hand towards me, but I pretended not to see. I, even after so many years, so much water under the bridge, didn't want to feel the touch of his hand.

May God forgive me.

Maurice took his hand instead, and he and Nurse Mulcahy helped him up the stairs to this room.

'This isn't my room,' he said.

'It's got a great view . . . a better view . . . the evening sun, Father. It's good to get the sun in the evening . . . and on stormy days you can smell the sea.'

He grunted. The sea meant little to him.

I had put an armchair by one of the windows so that he could sit there and look out towards the hills, read a bit if he wanted to, sleep; the doctor had said he would sleep a lot.

'And Nurse Mulcahy is next door.'

He grunted again. 'I thought I would have my own room.' His voice was like a fretful child.

'I think Mrs Quinlan's arrangements are very good.' Nurse Mulcahy moved him gently towards the chair as she spoke.

'Who is Mrs Quinlan?'

I laughed. 'I am Mrs Quinlan. I, Laura. You know that perfectly well.'

'Ah, yes,' he said as they lowered him gently into the chair. 'I could have seen the mill from my own room.'

'No sun. I thought you should have the benefit of the sun.'

And now, today, the sun shines through those windows and ignites the gold objects spread here before me, and silver, rubies, an emerald even, glitter in the light. He was a vain man; he was a peacock.

He brandished his charm and energy like a conjuror brandishes his brightly coloured silk scarves. People loved the flamboyant insincerity of my father; the smiles, the jokes, the promises flourished in front of their eyes; sleight of hand, magic tricks.

Even then, when he came to us that day to die, he had his own teeth, a fine thick head of hair, and eyes that were still, from time to time, a most shocking blue.

The next time Dominic O'Hara came to visit her it was raining. She heard the jangle of the bell and put her book down. She wondered for a moment if she would leave whoever it was there on the doorstep.

The bell jangled again.

Page one seventy.

'Someone had told him that Enrico Caruso could shatter a vase with the power of his voice, and he had spent years trying to imitate him, even with the window panes.'

Page one seven o. She put the book on the table and got up.

A wisp of smoke had escaped from the fire and tickled at the back of her throat. East wind, she thought.

The bell jangled again.

She moved across the room.

No one visited her.

She was not presumed to be part of the visiting circuit. Standoffish.

Snobby.

Cold.

Different.

Indifferent.

Protestant.

Whatever?

Not someone to be dropped in on.

The rain drummed on the glass dome over the stairwell and the bell jangled again.

She ran the last couple of steps, and remembered how she used to jump down the last three steps . . . sometimes four, five, six. . . .

'Laura . . .' her mother's voice wailed in her head. 'The house will fall down.'

'Oh.'

She opened the door and saw Dominic huddled into his anorak, his hair darkened by the rain was plastered to his head.

He stepped into the hall, brushing past her, not waiting for an invitation.

'What a day.'

He spoke the words, then shook himself for a moment like a dog just out of the sea; drops spattered from him onto the floor. He took off his coat and looked around for somewhere to put it and then threw it onto one of the ornately carved hall chairs.

'Do come in,' she said, closing the door.

He smiled slightly. 'Do you mind . . . ?'

'I'll make some tea.' She moved towards the kitchen.

His feet slap-slapped behind her on the flags.

Father's feet made no sound when he came up behind her; his shoes were neat, well fitting, highly polished. In this dark corner between the dining room door and the passage to the kitchen, he could catch at her shoulder or her arm before she was even aware of his presence.

'Don't bother about tea.'

She turned round and smiled at him.

'It's no bother. I'd be having some myself, anyway.'

'You said I could come. I hope. . . .'

'That's all right.'

'I hope . . . I don't want to barge in. I saw Mr Quinlan heading off in his car and I thought . . . well . . .'

'He's gone up to Dublin to a meeting.'

'This is the moment. That's what I thought . . . to go up and have a look round . . . you know, at . . . see you, actually. I thought it would be nice to see you. . . .'

'I'm delighted.'

'. . . again.'

'I'll make tea. You know where my sitting room is. Go on up. I'll be after you in a few minutes.'

She walked quickly down the dark passage to the kitchen.

'I mustn't run. I have to stop running.'

Behind her she heard his feet on the stairs . . . slap-slap. Two at a time he was running up them, like a schoolboy.

The lid of the kettle on the Aga was rattling gently.

Will he stay long?

What will I say to him? Or he to me?

I don't mind listening. For a short while I am prepared to listen.

I don't want to be forced to talk. I hate talking.

I don't want to smile and smile and nod my head and smile again.

I will give him tea and wait in silence.

When she went into the sitting room with the tray, he was standing by the window with a tiny jade frog in his hand. He was peering at the perfection of detail, holding it up to the light, intent on the shadings, green and grey, dark, light, moving, changing as the light changed.

He held it out towards her. 'This. Tell me about this.'

'My great-grandfather collected jade. He travelled in China. He spent most of his life travelling.'

She put the tray on a table. 'Hats, fans, kimonos, parasols, jade, porcelain, ivory, paintings, toys . . . you know those little nodding men . . . wonderful, tiny nodding men. I have fifteen of them in my bedroom. Each one quite different to the others.'

'Empire building. That's what Mr Quinlan said.'

She shook her head. 'Oh, no. He was just a traveller. He was lucky, my great-grandmother was able to keep things going here. There was the mill, you know. He didn't fancy sitting here being a miller. My mother used to say that there wasn't a country in the world he hadn't been to. He had this man . . . well, servant I suppose, called Markey, who seemed to have the same notions in *his* head and they both spent all their time travelling. They came home from time to time and their wives had babies nine months later. Both of them.'

She laughed. 'I always used to think that was funny . . . all those little Markeys and all those little Hansons, almost like twins. And their mothers, managing. Weren't women amazing, that they could cope with all that? Such strength. I envy them that strength. It would have been easy enough, I suppose, for my great-grandmother, but I often used to wonder if Mrs Markey hated my great-grandfather for taking her husband away like that.'

'Probably not,' he said. 'Think of all the babies she'd have had if he'd been here all the time.'

She poured two cups of tea.

'I'm sorry,' she said. 'I'm chattering. I hate people who chatter. Milk?'

'Mr Quinlan said empire building.'

'Maurice isn't always right, you know. He has odd notions about my family. My father was the same. Maurice never listens when you tell him things. He just shuts his ears to what he doesn't want to hear.'

She waved the milk jug in his direction.

'Just a drop,' he said.

Carefully he put the frog back on the shelf, in its space among so many other jade objects: leaping fish, an old man weighted down by a sack on his shoulders, a dog scratching its ear, a man reading, a woman bending down, a child laughing, a child crying; some pale, almost white, others a deep, glowing green.

She stood, not quite sure what to do; she felt off balance somehow, as if she were no longer in her own room.

'Aren't you going to sit down?' he asked. 'Have some tea? Relax? You look like you're about to fly away. Don't do that.'

She nodded and poured some tea into a cup for herself and went and sat down in her armchair by the fire. He moved across the room and sat down opposite her, his legs stretched out in front of him, the cup and saucer tilting dangerously in his hand.

He never took his eyes off her. He was examining

her as he had examined the frog; lights, shades, the carved intricacies of her body.

'Yes,' he said.

'What?'

'Sorry,' he said. 'I was just mumbling.'

'What do you do?' he asked after a very long silence.

'Well. . . .' Her voice was cautious. 'I pass the time. Why do you want to know? I am a wife. I don't do anything. Yes . . . pass the time.'

'People say you never go out.'

'I garden.'

'You know what I mean.'

'I suppose you could say that I guard this house, this mad museum. I am the curator of my ancestor's folly. Does that answer your question? I don't like being cross-examined.'

'I'm sorry,' he said. 'I didn't mean to do that. I'm just curious, that's all. I just wondered about you . . . about your life.'

She didn't speak.

'Curiosity killed the cat,' he said after a while. Then he drank the tea in his cup in one long gulp.

'Sometimes I have to do things for Maurice . . . meet people, that sort of thing. Give dinner parties. I have to do that. It really wouldn't be . . . well . . . fair, if I didn't. But I'm all right here, you know. On my own. People are right, I don't go out. Not like other people go out. I don't. . . .' Her fingers pulled at each other, fighting against the black of her skirt. ' . . . feel the need.'

He waited in silence.

'I am afraid.'

'What of?'

'I am afraid of my father.'

'Isn't your father dead?'

'Yes.'

'Ghost . . . spirit?'

She shook her head.

'There are times,' she said, 'I feel his hands around my neck.'

She looked up and across the room at him and laughed.

'I'm sorry. I shouldn't have said such a thing to you. Such a daft thing. It's no wonder people think I'm a little gone in the head. You see, one of the reasons I don't like talking to people is . . . things like that just come popping out of my mouth, unasked. People don't like that . . . do they? They like words, thoughts they can understand. Wouldn't you agree? People, by and large, don't like to be disturbed. Now, if you want to have a look round, carry on. I will read my book.'

She picked up the book from the arm of the chair where she had left it when she heard the bell ring, and opened it at page 170.

'Carry on,' she repeated, and turned her eyes to the book.

'He liked nothing better than to sing at funerals. He had the voice of a galley slave, untrained but capable of impressive registers. Someone had told him that Enrico Caruso. . . .'

'They wanted, longed, prayed for me to have a vocation. Become, you understand, a priest. They called me Dominic. That . . .'

'. . . could shatter a vase with the power of his voice. . . .'

'. . . was the gift they gave me at birth, like some parents have been known to give a newborn baby a Stradivarius, or a kingdom; I was given that name. . . .'

'. . . and he had spent years trying to imitate him. . . .'

– 25 –

'. . . and all the weight of their unthwartable expectations.'

'. . . even with the window panes.'

'Are you listening?'

'His friends brought him the most delicate vases they had come across in their travels through the world. . . .'

'Were you an only child?' She asked the question without raising her head from the book.

'No. No. One of five. A brother and three sisters.'

A log fell from the fire onto the hearth, spraying sparks and a bitter smell of smoke.

She carefully put aside the book and knelt down to deal with the situation.

'And your brother and sisters . . . are they also. . . .'

'No. I was the chosen victim.'

She looked round at him, startled by the words, startled by the sourness of his voice.

Rain was starting to whip the window, and some drops landed down the chimney, making the fire spit angrily.

'My brother Kieron is the director of investments in a merchant bank in London. He serves Mammon with a magnificent Thatcherite enthusiasm. As I was supposed to serve God.'

'How do your parents feel about that?'

'Oh . . . they were delighted, quite delighted and proud. My father never stops talking about him. My mother's dead.' He paused for a moment and then repeated the words.

'My mother's dead.'

'I. . . .'

'She died.'

'I'm sorry.'

'About a year ago. Yes, almost. May. At home. She was lucky enough to die at home. I . . . ah. . . .'

He cleared his throat, swallowed mucus that had gathered there.

'We all gathered round her bed and I was . . . I was . . . just . . . I spoke the words of the Act of Contrition and they spoke the words with me, softly, letting my voice lead them, and she died, just quite quietly . . . beautifully, one of my sisters said. I actually didn't know she was dead until one of them told me. Lena. Lena was the one. She feels it is her duty to give bad news to people.'

'But are you a priest? Maurice didn't . . .'

'Three weeks after her funeral I told my father that I was leaving the priesthood. I do have to say that I wrote and told him. I am a coward by nature. They really only recognise success. They wanted us to be able to move easily in places of power. It never occurred to either of them that I might end up as a classics teacher. A recusant classics teacher at that.'

He laughed.

'Classics! A good training for the brain, so they say. That's what he said to me when I told him I wanted to study classics. I really wanted to explore an unpolluted language . . . and teach. I like to teach. He thought I would climb on the cold branches of Greek and Latin to the top of some tree. "My son, the monsignor. . . ."'

'I hate it when people talk like this. . . .'

'I'm sorry. It's as you said; when lonely people start to talk, weird things come popping out. I'm also very good at rugby. I might well have played for Ireland, if I'd not had my nose to the grindstone.'

He suddenly got up from the chair with an exuberance that tumbled his half-empty cup to the floor. It didn't break, but tea and tea leaves spread across the pale carpet.

'Oh, drat! I am so sorry. I am a clumsy oaf. Let

me. . . .' He pulled a handkerchief from his pocket and bent down and dabbed.

'It's all right,' she said. 'I'll get a cloth.'

'Never worry. Look. Behold. The great thing is to catch it at once. I am always spilling things. I am a clumsy oaf. Look. Gone. Good as new.'

He looked at his wet handkerchief, rolled it up, and with a surprisingly violent gesture, threw it into the fire. The fire hissed and spat with displeasure.

Laura laughed. 'Tell me,' she asked, 'if you'd had . . . well . . . the freedom. . . .' Gumption was the word she wanted to use. 'What would you have chosen to do? Be a classics teacher?'

He shook his head. 'An actor.'

She laughed again, not sure whether to believe him or not.

He moved to the centre of the room and stood, the saucer in one hand, the cup dangling from the other, just gazing nowhere in particular, looking rather absurd, she thought.

> Build me a willow cabin at your gate,
> And call upon my soul within the house;
> Write loyal cantons of contemned love,
> And sing them, loud even in the dead of night;
> Holla your name to the reverberate hills,
> And make the babbling gossip of the air
> Cry out, Olivia! O you should not rest
> Between the elements of air and earth,
> But you should pity me.

The words settled, and then there was silence in which the fire still made angry noises.

'Yes,' she said.

He didn't move, still gazed into some past in his head.

'That's a woman's part,' she said.

'Well, of course, not really. Shakespeare wrote his women's parts for men to play. Viola is a woman played by a man playing at being a woman. Ambivalent, you might call it. Amby . . . valent.'

'I played Viola in the school play.'

'You must have had more courage then than you have now.'

'Yes. At sixteen I had courage. Yes. I spoke those lines in a high, fluting voice. Like a choirboy might speak them. Well, that's what I thought at the time. Nice play. I loved it. I wore a purple velvet outfit, I remember that. I think I may have it somewhere still.'

'How old are you now?'

She didn't answer.

'I do apologise. Do you mind my asking?'

'Of course not. Thirty-seven. Twenty-one years since I was Viola in the school play.'

'I'd have another cup of tea.'

He put the cup carefully on the saucer and held it out towards her.

'It'll be cold.'

'No matter.'

She poured it out and he drank it back, there and then, with a dramatic flourish.

'Disgusting,' he said, putting the cup and saucer down on the table.

She laughed. 'You're a clown.'

'I'm a teacher.'

'A priest.' He said nothing.

'Once a priest, always a priest, so they say. The rain has stopped,' she said, looking past him out of the window. Shadows of clouds hurried over the hillside.

She wished he would go. She wished the sound of his voice would leave the room. She wished for silence. When she looked back to where he had been standing, he had gone.

For a moment she wondered whether she had imagined his presence, in which case, she muttered angrily to herself, I really am going potty, but then she heard the sharp sounds of steps in the hall below. The hall door opened and slammed shut.

After storms, seaweed lies on the beach, great piles of glutinous ribbons, leaves, bunches of grape-like fruit, sea ferns, all tumbled together by the movement of the waves. Men used to come with horses and carts when I was a child, and load it up and take it away to spread on the fields, and the beach would be clean again, and the air would be free of the heavy, repellent smell. Now the men come with tractors and they leave the scars of their wheels on the hill at the back of the beach, and they also leave behind them the detritus of the world that is today's sea wrack; plastic containers of all shapes and sizes, rusty tins, broken glass, usually smoothed by the action of the sea, and bags; I have seen red, blue, yellow bags, black bags and white bags with names of stores printed on them in weatherproof writing. Oil drums, shoes, and sometimes the decomposing bodies of sea birds, their feathers coated with oil.

'I would love to have been a pirate,' my mother said to me one winter's day, as we stood on the dunes above the beach and watched the crashing waves devouring the land, beating, sucking gnawing, always, it seemed, winning. 'Like Grace O'Malley'.

She always walked with long strides and I scurried beside her. Her eyes seemed to embrace everything, the birds, the floating weed, the distant hull of a ship on the horizon, trailing smoke; she also trailed smoke; she devoured cigarettes as we walked, lighting each one furiously from the stub of the last. She would look at each one with hatred as she took it from the packet. Her fingers and the nails of the first and second fingers of her right hand were stained brown.

'Dangerous,' I said to her.

Even then I wasn't one for danger.

She laughed. 'Such freedom.' Smoke trailed from her lips as she spoke.

'Daddy fought for freedom,' I said.

She laughed, and then turned and strode along the top of the dune. The sound of her laughter was blown back towards me as I hurried after her.

'Don't you believe it.' Her words and the smoke and the sound of her laughter reached back to me.

'That's what he always says. Fought for freedom and won. He says that, too.'

'Daddy fought for Daddy.'

I must have been about ten. It's hard to say; memory is like a kaleidoscope, repatterning, retricking the past in your head.

I didn't believe her when she said those words. I never really knew when to believe her.

Daddy's room was filled with the proofs of his honesty: flags, badges, a bandoleer hanging on the wall by the door, photographs of statesmen and heroes, photographs of Daddy shaking hands with heroes, Daddy with his arm casually slung round the shoulder of a hero, Daddy, young, handsome, full of the glory of his own heroism.

So how could I believe her?

I found a bone in the bent grass. It was dazzling white, the shoulder blades of a rabbit probably, picked by the wind and scavenging birds, and I brought it home for him.

Maybe it wasn't that same day; maybe I wasn't yet ten.

I stood by the door of his room for a moment, listening to the low murmur of voices inside, male voices as always, male voices. I knocked and the sound of the voices stopped; there was a laugh and I heard my father's steps coming across the room to the door.

He opened it and looked down at me. He seemed very tall.

'Laura?'

I held the shining bone out towards him.

'This is for you.'

The smell of smoke and whiskey drifted from the room.

'For me, pet?'

'I found it on the sand hills.'

'It's beautiful, so it is.'

He took it from my fingers. 'Little pet. What a little pet you are.'

He put his hand on my head, fingers deep into my hair, and pulled me into the room.

Two men were sitting by the fire.

'This is my little Laura.'

They smiled at me. One raised his glass in my direction.

'My little pet who brings me presents.' He held the bone up towards them.

I blushed, and his fingers pressed even deeper, almost into my skull.

He took his hand away and gave me a pat on the shoulder.

'Run along now, there's a good girl. Daddy's talking business.'

Now when I walk on the beach, I walk alone. I no longer have to scurry; I can take my own pace; stride or stand or crouch down scooping through the shells with my fingers, looking for precious cowries.

In the summer children come and swim, and at weekends families picnic in the grass above the beach. I have put notices up on the paths that lead to the shore.

PLEASE TAKE YOUR LITTER HOME WITH YOU.

Maurice was angry when I did that.

He said I had no right to bully people like that. 'Arrogant' was the word he used.

I agreed with him. It was an arrogant gesture, but I did it just the same. No one has complained.

Most people take their litter home.

'Just half a dozen, dote.'

They ate in the kitchen when there were no visitors.

The table, a leftover from the past, was long and pale and well scrubbed. Around them, machines purred and ticked and blinked when encouraged to.

'Six.'

'Six,' she repeated.

'With us, of course.'

'Of course. Yes.' She laughed. 'Mustn't forget us.'

'Six isn't much of a party. Can you think of anyone else? Anyone suitable?'

She shook her head.

'Of course not.' His voice was faintly sarcastic.

'You decide. You tell me.'

'I'll ask Sandra Mooney . . . she's O'Brien's right-hand woman. A whizzer. Nice, though, and going places.'

Laura nodded. 'Seven. With us.'

'And what about that Mr O'Hara?'

'Why on earth . . .'

'O'Brien's one of the rugby selectors. It'd be great if we could get him down to visit the school. Madame Poulenc is Greek. . . . Didn't he say he spoke Greek?'

'Classical . . .'

'That's great. That's fixed. Eight, then. With us.'

She knew by the look on his face that he had already asked the whizzer and Dominic.

He looked at his watch. 'My God, is that the time?'

He pushed his chair back and stood up, dropping his napkin from his knees onto the floor.

'The Union are holding a meeting on new EEC regulations on additives in foodstuffs. I said I'd be there.'

She knew by the look on his face that he was lying.

He came round the table and kissed her on the top of the head.

'Don't wait up, dote. I may have to have a few jars afterwards. You know the way it is.'

'Yes.'

He rubbed at the side of her neck with a finger. His hand smelled fragrant.

She sat quite still, didn't move a muscle.

'Beautiful lady. Great lady. Lovely dote.'

She wanted to say, Go to hell, but instead she smiled at him.

'You'll be late for your meeting.'

The table was loaded, just the way he liked it to be, with flowers, silver, glass, candles flickering. He might sneer from time to time, but that was the way he liked it. He and Father had that in common; they each liked things to be done with style.

'*Bellissima*,' muttered Monsieur Poulenc. He took her hand and kissed it and his knee pressed against hers under the table.

'Cornubia,' she said. 'It is such a wonderful colour. I'm glad you like it.'

He looked taken aback.

'Glowing blood,' she said. 'As you said, *bellissima*.'

'Glaowing blut?'

'The flowers. Rhododendrons. Cornubia. It's one of the earlier flowering ones.' She moved her knee slightly away from his.

'Smoked saumon,' he said, turning his warm eyes towards his plate. 'They have right when they say Irish smoked saumon is the best of the world.'

Up at the other end of the table, Maurice leaned an ear towards Madame Poulenc, but his eyes were on Sandra Mooney.

Dominic O'Hara, dressed in a polo-necked shirt under his suit, pleated a slice of salmon onto his fork and shoved it into his mouth.

He looked up and caught her eye.

'Yes,' she said.

Dominic chewed ferociously and stared.

'We envy you zat.'

She laughed.

'You shouldn't. You have so much. You shouldn't want to have everything.'

The Frenchman looked pleased. '*Vous connaissez la France?*'

Dominic continued to stare at her. His eyes penetrated through her skull; she felt the touch of his eyes inside her brain. He took a large bite from a piece of brown bread and chewed ferociously again.

'Oh, yes,' she said. 'A bit. I know it a bit. I. . . .'

He was pleating the next slice of salmon. He looked hungry. She wondered if they didn't feed him adequately in the school. '. . . love France. I hid there for a year.'

M. Poulenc looked surprised. *'Pardon!* Hid?'

'Did I say that? How silly of me. Lived. I meant lived. *J'ai passé presque deux ans en France.* . . . That's what I meant to say.'

His hands were very neat. She watched him picking his way through the smoked salmon, the silver knife and fork balanced precisely in his fingers. A little touch of cayenne, a squeeze of lemon, just so. A little pat at his lips with the napkin as he chewed, and then a sip of wine.

Dominic's plate was empty and he twirled the stem of his glass in his fingers. He was not talking about rugby to Mr O'Brien.

'Yes,' she said. 'That was what I meant to say.'

'Comment?'

'It doesn't matter. I have forgotten all my French now. It's as if I had never been there. . . .'

'It would come back. You come with Maurice next time he come. It would be my great pleasure to help you with your recovery.'

'My recovery?'

'Of the language.'

She laughed. 'You are very kind. I never go with Maurice.'

'Why not?'

'I prefer to stay here.'

'A strange preference, if I may say. Perhaps unwise.' As he spoke he glanced up the table towards Miss Mooney.

'Perhaps,' she said coldly, and then leaned across the table.

'Mr O'Hara, do you know France? I'm sure you

know France. Help yourself to some wine and then tell us what you think of France.'

He held me by the shoulders and shook me.

I could hear the rattle of my feet on the floor as he shook and shook me.

'I warned you.' His voice sounded quite mad. 'Warned you.'

The hall was filled with light and darkness. I swung from light to darkness and my newly shorn head battered from side to side, not like my own clothed head but light, naked, another girl's head, another girl's feet rattling on the floor. But I could feel his fingers, cold with fury, through the sleeves of my dress, marking my skin. Suddenly he stopped shaking me. He didn't let go of my arms; indeed, if he had I think I would have fallen to the floor. We both stood struggling for breath, for words, and the dog barked at nothing out in the sunshine.

'Go to your room and calm yourself. We'll talk about this another time,' he said eventually.

Little by little his grip on my arms loosened.

The seam under my right arm had split.

'I'll do nothing you say. I will never. . . .'

'You're upset,' he said.

The dog still barked.

It was my mother's dog.

It had been my mother's dog.

He used to stand on the steps outside the front door and bark when he saw my mother's car turn in the gateway. He used to wait down on the little stone pier, and bark when her boat came flying in past the headland.

Now he was barking at nothing.

'You've torn my dress.'

He lifted his hands helplessly in the air.

'What matter?'

Everything had been said. The air around us was filled with bitter words; our heads were filled with bitter words. Hate, anger, blame, loathing, blame.

'You killed your mother,' he had said. 'I warned you. Warned you, warned you.'

I moved across the hall towards the stairs. As I passed him he put out a hand towards me, but I swerved and avoided his touch.

I don't remember packing.

I only remember the weight of my case and the way it dragged at my arm as I carried it down the steps later that day and put it into Mr O'Toole's taxicab.

I said goodbye to no one, not even the dog, sitting hopefully on the steps.

'A most successful evening, dote.'

She was brushing her heavy hair. A hundred strokes a day, Mother had always insisted on; it was now a habit.

The window was open and the night sounds had entered the silence of her room.

'God, it's freezing in here.'

He walked over and shoved the window down.

'How can you bear it?'

She put the hairbrush down on the dressing table. Her hair spun out round her as she moved, as if she were some Pre-Raphaelite damozel.

'I like it.'

'I don't like paying to heat the garden.'

He spoke the words automatically, without irritation.

She smiled.

He stood in the middle of the room, twirling the silk cord of his dressing gown round a finger and then untwirling it.

'Lovely dinner. Great. No one does a do like that better than you, dote. No one.'

'Thank you.'

'Tired?'

'So-so.'

He scratched for a moment at the top of his nose. His fingernails were orderly and shining slightly.

'Funny little Frog. He took a fancy to you.'

She picked up the brush and began slowly to brush her hair again. Seventy-eight, seventy-nine.

'Bright guy. Important. Yes. Useful would be a better word. Useful.'

He sat down on the edge of the bed. 'Wheels within wheels,' he said, just into the air.

He laughed suddenly. 'I must say, your man O'Hara isn't exactly filled with social graces. What do you think?'

'I couldn't understand why you asked him.'

'They say he's a spoiled priest. Have you heard that?'

'How would I hear that?' Eighty-nine, ninety.

'Something like that. A screwball, I'd say.'

I know what he wants to say, she thought. Her hair crackled suddenly under the brush.

I wish he'd say it and go, let me get to bed, let me be alone. Her hair crackled again and she threw the brush down onto the dressing table.

'Electricity,' she said.

He didn't hear her.

'Mmm. . . .' She yawned.

'Beautiful. You looked really beautiful. I could see that Poulenc was impressed. Whispering sweet nothings. . . .' His voice faded away.

He stood up abruptly and stood looking past her

at himself in the mirror. He still twirled at the silk cord. He had something on his mind.

'Bed. Bed, bed, bed. Mustn't keep you out of yours. Poor tired dote.' He came over and dropped a kiss from a height onto the top of her head. She never moved.

He took several steps towards the door.

'Oh, yes . . . I nearly forgot . . . Gerry and Maureen asked us up to stay for the weekend. Leopardstown. What do you think? I said I'd let them know first thing. . . . Madame Poulenc is dying to go racing.'

'How nice of them. . . .'

Let him sweat a bit, she thought.

'I haven't been to the races for ages. It might be fun.'

She turned away and watched him watching her, in the glass. The silver brush had her mother's initials twined on the back.

'I might get my hair cut. . . .'

'There won't be time.'

'Mmm. . . .' She yawned. 'I'll think about it, darling. I'll let you know at breakfast time.'

He nodded and moved towards the door again.

'No,' she said. 'No. I don't think I'll go. You go. I've got millions of things to do in the garden.'

'Are you sure?'

'I hate that sort of carry-on.'

'Don't be silly. Do come. We'll have a. . . .'

'No, thanks, Maurice. I'm all right here. I'm happy here. I feel like an unshelled snail when I go places like that . . . as if someone might stand on me at any moment.'

'Silly dote.' His voice had the confidence of relief in it. 'O.K., then. If you're sure. I'll give them a ring. . . . I'll make your. . . .'

'Yes, please do that.'

'Goodnight, dote.'

After he had closed the door she crossed the room and pushed open the window. The cool air embraced her. She turned off the light and stood in the darkness by the window and listened to the night breathing and stirring, the wind strumming at the branches that any day now would come into leaf.

It was a warm weekend.

The early midges were out in their millions. She wore a red scarf tied round her hair and a long-sleeved shirt over her jeans, but still they managed to get through to her flesh and torment her.

At about half past four she threw the hook with which she had been clearing brambles down on the ground and yelled.

'Piss off, bastards.'

The air quivered with their almost invisible wings.

In a sheltered corner, way down below the house, someone about a hundred years before had built a summerhouse. It had for a long time been charming and private, a dolls' house almost, with long windows and a carved wooden balcony, hidden in the fold of a small hill and with a stream singing through tall trees.

Since the drowning of her mother, Laura had not been near it. She had watched from a distance as brambles and ferns grew and shrubs became choked and the unpruned branches of the trees thickened out and finally the little house also was drowned. The notion of clearing the corner had arrived in her mind one morning not long after her father's funeral. It had been like a letter flopping through the letterbox onto the floor; she had picked it up and looked at it for a while, she had put the notion aside, like a bill she hadn't wanted to pay, and finally after several weeks she had opened the envelope and contemplated the contents with surprise and pleasure.

'I think I'll clear the corner down by the stream,' she said to Maurice at lunch one day.

'Uhhun.'

'Rediscover the old summerhouse.'

'What summerhouse?'

'There used to be a summerhouse down there, in among all that mess.'

'I don't remember a summerhouse.'

'I don't suppose you would. It was gone . . . hidden . . . swallowed, long before you came to live here. The year I came back from France, you could only see a wee bit of the roof through the mess.'

'Why bother? If you want a summerhouse I'll get some of the men to build you one next winter.'

'Curiosity killed the cat.'

'It'll be a ghastly job and I can't spare any of the men at the moment.'

'I'll do it.'

'If you wait till the autumn . . .'

'Penance.'

'What does that mean?'

'The performance of some act of self-mortification as an expression of penitence. I looked the word up in the dictionary.'

'I know what the word means,' he said crossly. 'I mean in relation to you. Penance! Are you thinking of turning?'

She burst out laughing.

'No,' she said. 'I'm just thinking of disinterring the past . . . a little bit of the past.'

'I can't stop you, but it'll be a hell of a lot of hard work for nothing.'

'I was just putting you in the picture.'

'The past's a waste of time. We should all forget about the bloody past.'

'There's a stream down there. I might make a water garden.'

'You do what you want.'

'Yes, I will.'

She picked up the rake to rake the cut branches and the brambles into a pile for burning; a bonfire would discourage the midges.

She already had the basis of the fire, paper, dry twigs, a few light branches to establish it, and then a pile of weeds, brambles, ferns, dry grass, and bits of timber and other rubbish that she had come across as she worked.

She lit a match and pushed it into the centre of the structure. It flickered for a moment and went out. A little wisp of smoke hung for a moment in the air and then was gone. She knelt down and pulled a corner of the paper towards her and lit it; the flame ran along the paper to where the dry sticks were balanced together, yellow and blue running flame caught at more paper, and then a stick cracked; a flare of dry grass and the flames started to climb up into the structure.

'Bravo,' said a voice.

Startled, she looked round.

Dominic was standing behind her. He appeared to be wearing the same clothes he had worn two nights before at the dinner party.

'Oh, hello.' Her voice was quite unwelcoming.

'I knew you couldn't be far away. The house was like the *Marie Céleste* . . . doors open, machines humming, bread and butter on the kitchen table. The radio was on, for God's sake, blaring music.

Like a Red Indian, I tracked you down. Clever, don't you think?'

She got up and threw a branch onto the fire.

'Do you mind? Are you angry with me? Your face is bleeding.'

'Brambles.' She put up a hand and felt the scrawb on her cheek. 'They are very vengeful. I'm always finding ghastly thorns and scrapes in the most surprising places. No, I'm not cross. Just taken aback. I wasn't expecting to see anyone real.'

'Do you mind? Will I go away?'

She shook her head.

'I could help. I don't know what you're up to, but you look as if you could do with some help.'

'Help by all means if you want to. Keep that fire going and I'll collect some more stuff.'

'I was at a loose end.' He picked up a pile of branches and carried them to the fire. 'So. . . .'

She had disappeared.

'So. . . .'

'That's what Maurice said the first day you came.'

She came out from the undergrowth, pulling a large branch behind her.

'He said you were at a loose end.'

'I suppose I must have been. I don't remember. But if Maurice said so. . . .'

'Maurice is not always wholly truthful.'

'Let me give you a hand with that.'

'Put it on the fire. There's lots more for burning in there. Just take care when you're pulling it out. I think there's some good stuff in under all that mess. I'm treading softly at the moment.'

He pulled the branch well out of the undergrowth and heaved it onto the fire.

Sour, grey smoke was forming a mushroom cloud; flames hungrily ate the twigs. Sparks leaped as the branch crashed onto the fire.

'How much of this are you clearing?'

'The lot. Right down to the stream. Somewhere in there is a summerhouse. It's hard to believe, I know. All sorts of lovely trees, too. I remember one of those magnolias with bell-like flowers and a wonderful smell. I can't remember the name.'

'Choked by now, I'd say.'

He picked up the fork and began to turn the outer brambles in towards the centre of the fire.

'I do hope not. My mother planted it when she was first married. The wedding tree, she used to call it.'

She disappeared again into the undergrowth.

'A symbolic gesture,' Mother said.

She clipped a twig with her secateurs and handed it, with its drooping, bell-like flower, to me.

'Smell.'

Such sweetness.

Every May she did the same thing. Clipped a twig and handed it to me, spoke the same words.

I never could make out if she had forgotten that she had said those words before, or if it was part of a ritual for her. I had the sense not to speak. I took the twig and smelled the flower in silence.

'The wedding tree.'

If it was raining, the flower would be decorated with trembling pearls and the smell would be diminished. I remember my surprise and disappointment when that happened for the first time.

'Still going strong,' she would say then. 'Amen.'

They worked in tolerable silence for about an hour.

Close to the fire the midges were discouraged by the smoke, but back in the undergrowth they attacked with terrible vigour.

'I can't take it another second.'

She pulled a tangle of brambles and branches behind her.

'I'm destroyed.'

'It's lucky you never felt the need to be an explorer.'

'Sure is.'

Together they piled the fire high and then stood back to watch the flames catch.

'I found a palm tree.'

'What a strange thing to find.'

She shook her head.

'No. I remembered when I came across it that she had planted two, and a camellia. . . . I'd say that'll be dead by now, but the palm trees will recover. This one doesn't look too bad. Come and I'll show you.'

She held her hand out towards him and he took it and they walked silently through the ferns and the rough grass, ducking the low branches as they went. The palm tree stood about ten feet tall. Its trunk was straight and bare for about six feet and then it burst into a series of complicated patterns of leaves and branches, spirals, whorls, whirls. Bushes and undergrowth had almost smothered it, but now it was free.

'It's like Christmas.'

They stood still, holding hands.

'Presents, you know.' She said the words in case he hadn't understood. He nodded.

'I want to find and find and find as quickly as possible. Is that greedy?'

She suddenly became aware of his hand in hers and let it go. She put her hand into the pocket of her jeans.

'God, I'm hot and sticky,' she said. 'Let's go and have a cup of tea.'

As they pushed their way back under the branches she kept both hands clenched in her pockets. He walked behind her with docility.

They collected the rakes and the hook and secateurs and walked up the hill towards the house.

'Do you disapprove of my leaving the radio on? Maurice does. He thinks I am extraordinarily extravagant. I usually have reasons for the things I do, but he. . . . I hate going into a silent house. I like to be welcomed into a house by friendly sounds.'

'I don't disapprove. I was merely surprised. I expected to find you behind each door . . . or Mr Quinlan. . . .'

'He's away. He's in Dublin at the races. You knew that though, didn't you?'

'I. . . .'

'Everyone here knows everything. I don't suppose you're any exception.'

She turned and looked at him.

His face was red.

'Sorry,' she said.

She handed him the hook and the secateurs.

'Here. Put these in the porch. I'm going to run up and have a bath. There's a shower in the cloakroom if you want one. I feel so sticky. A mess. Can you make tea?'

'Do you want me to go?'

'Of course you can make tea. You know where the kitchen is. Make tea.'

She toed off her espadrilles and left them by the hall door.

'C'est ton époux, ton époux fidèle. . . .' a voice sang from the kitchen.

She walked across the hall.

- 47 -

The voice was rich and deep.

'*Entends ma voix qui t'appèlle.*'

At the bottom of the stairs she turned back to him.

'See what I mean,' she said. 'How great it is to come into a house that is singing that to you.' She laughed. 'You look like a statue. . . . *The Man from the Fields.*'

She moved up the stairs.

'Have you lost your tongue?' she said.

'*J'ai perdu mon Eurydice. . . .*'

'I'll tell you something no one knows. I don't know why I'm telling you. Maybe it's the music. I killed my mother.'

She was gone across the landing.

A door shut.

'*Rien égale mon malheur. . . .*'

He dropped the gardening tools onto the floor of the porch and took his handkerchief from his pocket. His face was sweating. Salt stung his eyes, and snail trails of sweat almost like tears trickled down his cheek and over his jaw. He stepped into the hall; her shoes lay on the floor by his feet.

'*Mortel silence! Vaine espérance!*'

He wiped at his face with the white folded handkerchief that was clean and pressed from the matron's ironing board.

'*Quel tourment déchire mon coeur!*'

Why?

Why did I say that?

The spinnaker was chevronned, red and blue.

I have never said such a thing before.

I have never really brought to the front of my mind such a possibility.

They brought the sail up to the house that after-noon in September.

They laid it out on the grass in front of the house and we stood and looked down at it.

Chevronned red and blue.

Father nodded, and then turned and went towards the house.

The chestnut trees were turning orange.

Chevronned red and blue.

The dog sat on the steps in front of the hall door, silent.

I put my hand into the pocket of my skirt and felt her ring.

I wished I too were dead.

At the door my father paused for a moment and spoke two words over his shoulder.

'Thanks, lads.'

I lie in the water; my hair floats, stirs.

They never found her body.

A spar, some timbers, a rope washed up on the beach.

Why did I say that to him?

The cable for the television aerial taps against the window.

I must get that fixed.

When I close my eyes, I see blue and red chev-rons.

Why did I speak such a lie?

My hair floats, stirs.

She ran straight upon the rocks, they said; the hull was torn like paper, they said.

The sea would have licked, picked at the pins in her hair, spread her hair wide, picked her clean, sucked the flesh from her bones; I see nails, eyes, flesh, rings, watch, jeans, jersey, shoes, socks, and all those things that I had said to her picked clean from her brain. Oceaned forever away.

I sit up and the water runs from my hair down over my body and I grope over the side of the bath for towels.

Did I kill her?

Did he kill her?

If I had kept that secret . . .

If, if. . . .

If. . . .

The evening sun came in sideways through the kitchen windows. He had put two mugs on the table, and milk and the bowl of sugar lumps, a jar of raspberry jam, some butter; as she came into the room, he was busy cutting slices from a great wheel of brown bread.

'I'm starving,' he said. 'I hope you don't mind . . . ?'

'Go ahead. Cut some for me, too.'

She took the teapot from the top of the Aga and put it on the table.

She sat down. Her head was wrapped in a large yellow turban of towel.

'You smell good,' he said. 'Rich.'

She unfastened the towel and began to rub at her hair.

'I am rich.'

He spread some butter on a slice of bread and then raspberry jam, thickly, as a child might do it, and put it on a plate in front of her. He poured out two cups of tea. He sat down opposite her at the table and watched her.

'I miss this sort of domesticity,' he said after a long silence. 'Such simple areas of peace.'

'If you had remained in the priesthood, you would presumably have had compensations.'

She folded the towel in two, and leaning back in her chair, hung it over the rail in front of the Aga.

'Spiritual compensations.'

He laughed.

The sun began its descent behind the black hill; slowly the room would become grey, but now, at this moment, glass glittered, cups on the dresser glittered, pans hanging on the wall above the stove glittered, and a fly, one of last summer's leftovers, buzzed on the windowpane, longing to be out in the brilliant air.

'You look like an Italian painting, with your hair all fizzy like that. Giovanni Bellini, *Madonna. . . .*'

'*Madonna Eating a Piece of Bread and Jam.*'

'Why have you no child?'

She didn't answer, just chewed at the bread and jam.

'I'm sorry . . . was that overstepping the . . . ?'

'No . . . that's O.K. It was obviously not in God's plan for me.'

She put the bread down on the plate and dabbled at the corner of her mouth with a finger, removing crumbs.

'Don't think I don't mind. I do. I bloody mind. That's what most people think, you know, Maurice's family, and so on . . . they think I don't want children. Poor Maurice, that awful wife of his doesn't want children. Reject, reject, reject . . . that's all my body used to do.'

'Used to do?'

'Yes. That's what I said. Did you have a shower?'

'Oh . . . yes . . . I . . . yes. . . . Thank you. I had a . . . lovely hot water. At the school the water's never really hot. Never pleasurably hot.'

'You should talk to Maurice about it. Isn't he chairman or something?'

'I think it's intentional.'

'Moral fibre?'

'Something like that.'

'Pleasure is sin?'

He laughed.

'More likely to be economic fibre.'

'I suppose so.'

'Some more bread?'

She shook her head.

'I'm nearly forty,' she said.

The sunlight moved up the wall behind her.

'I have nothing. I am no one. I am weightless, sightless. I only see this woman running. She wears black and she runs. I see myself running, weightless. I am nearly. . . .'

He must have moved and she stopped talking. She looked across the table at him, now becoming grey in the greyness.

'. . . forty.'

She smiled for a moment.

'You see, Maurice isn't exactly the sort of person you can say something like that to. See a doctor, that's what he would say. An expert. The best. Sometimes I think they would lock me up. I am already in prison. It would have to be the best. Maurice always goes for the best. Poor Maurice. I think he thought he was getting some sort of best when he got me. Instead he got a broken reed. I find that quite funny at times.'

She leaned forward and peered at him.

'I can't see your face any longer. Are you disgusted with me?'

'No.'

'That's O.K., then.'

'I presume that thing you said . . . earlier on . . . you know . . . about your mother . . . I presume . . . ?'

'I honestly don't know. I thought I had asked her for help and instead she went out and ran her boat on the rocks. Her body was never found, so nothing was ever finished. No rituals, no – I was going to say full stop, but you can't say that really, can you? There can never be a full stop, a moment when you can say "End of Story." I believe in all that singing and dancing at the graveside, funeral baked meats, all that carry-on. If you don't have that you can't believe that death has happened. I never felt my mother had died, merely that she had unkindly abandoned me.'

'Why would she do a thing like that?'

'I suppose because I burdened her with demands she felt she couldn't handle. I thought she had such strength, such power.'

She laughed.

'I hadn't reached the age when you can look dispassionately at your parents, see them as people rather than angels or devils.'

'Maybe it was an accident.'

She shook her head. She held her right hand out across the table towards him.

'See,' she said.

In the dimness he could see she wore a heavy gold ring in which was set an oval red seal.

'That.'

'The ring?'

'She always wore it. No matter what she was doing or where she was going she wore that. It was like part of her body; it had belonged to her father and his father and so on.'

He looked at her hand stretched out towards him on the table and wondered whether to touch it, but

as he wondered she pulled her hand back and
stared down at the ring.

'I found it on the table beside her bed.'

I stood outside her bedroom door.

I half believed, even after a week, that if I
turned the handle and went in I would find her
there, sitting in the armchair by the window,
reading, or perhaps writing letters at the little
desk that had belonged to her mother before
her.

'Darling,' she would say, 'I'll be with you in a
tick.' Those were the words she always used. She
hated the privacy of her room invaded.

I would sit on the chair outside the door and wait
for her to come out to me or call me in.

I would listen to the slight movements coming
from the room; a drawer being opened, shoes clattering on the floor, a cough perhaps, sometimes a
little ripple of song. But now all I could hear were
the murmuring voices of Father and Mr Byrne, the
solicitor, rising up the stairwell from my father's
study on the floor below.

I tapped nervously on the door and then turned
the handle.

The room was stuffy.

She would have hated that. I went over to the
window and opened it. She liked open windows,
fresh air, windy days, good sailing days. They were
the sort of days she liked best. Her nightdress and
dressing gown were folded on the end of the bed,
her slippers below on the floor, as she always expected to find them.

Brushes, combs, jars, bottles, pots waited in their
places on her dressing table.

She was neat and orderly. Scents, creams, lotions, oils.

She was also vain.

No harm in vanity.

'Mummy?' A foolish, whispered question.

I opened the big wardrobe and the smell of her clothes made my eyes prickle.

'Mummy. Mum?'

She hated that word. Hated to be called that. If she were there, she would react to that.

I wanted to pull back the bedclothes and climb into her bed, cover myself with her sheets, bury my head in her pillows and then hear her scandalised voice reproving me.

It was at that moment I saw the ring and I thought, It's all right, she's only gone out for a while, she'll be back to get her ring. She'll be back, sure enough.

I picked it up and felt its cold abandonment in the palm of my hand. I felt that cold reaching into me.

I put the ring into my pocket and went to her dressing table.

Her mother's silver hand glass, heavy and decorated with twined initials and flowers, lay among the other objects on the table. I picked it up, balanced its weight in my hand, and hurled it through the top half of the window.

Glass cascaded, sprayed, like a torrent of raindrops, and I could hear the tinkling of the shards on the path below.

A door below opened and footsteps hurried on the stairs.

'What . . . what . . . what?' My father's question bounced around my head.

I watched him in the mirror.

A tall, handsome man . . . a touch of grey over

his ears, his face a little too red, like a man who had been too long in the sun.

'What . . . what . . . Laura . . . is it?'

Behind him, Mr Byrne peered nervously into the room.

'Tck tck tck.' He sounded always like a grandfather clock.

I didn't turn round.

I just stared at them both in the glass.

'Tck tck tck. . . .'

It was my mother who had said, 'He sounds just like a grandfather clock. I wonder if he has a weekly or a monthly balance.' I remember laughing when she said that.

'Are you all right? What happened?'

My father approached me, his arms outstretched.

'I broke the window.'

'Window? Broke . . . but . . . why . . . window . . . but why, pet?'

I moved sideways to avoid his touch. Broken glass crackled under my feet.

'There's glass everywhere. Why? That's what I ask. Why? Don't move, Mick. Don't come another step in.'

'Tck tck tck.'

'What in the name of all that's holy did you do that for?'

'She's dead.'

'Tck tck tck.'

He leaned out of the window and looked down at the hand glass lying on the path, at the shining, sparkling glass.

'She wouldn't have liked you to do that.'

He pulled his head back into the room again as he spoke and turned round towards me.

'That was one of her precious objects.'

'Tck tck tck.'

'You know how she valued her precious things. I hope you're not going to let us all down. . . .' His voice was threatening. '. . . by going to pieces. By making a show of yourself.'

That, of course, I thought, wasn't exactly what he meant.

The colour of the sky was brighter through the starred break in the window. Jagged daggers of glass sparked in the sun.

'We have to keep our suffering to ourselves. We do. People like us. That's what she would want. Laura. Laura, say something.'

I just kept on staring at him in the glass.

'Yes.'

It was the thin voice of Mr Byrne.

He took a small, careful step into the room as he spoke.

'My dear Laura, she is, alas, dead. We have to suppose that, um, yes, she is dead. Tck tck. Mrs Byrne and I. . . .'

'Well, if she's dead . . . like you say . . . and Father thinks, if she's um tick tick dead . . . I only hope she's in a better place than this world. I think this world is bloody.'

'Laura!'

'Bloody. Fucking bloody.'

'Laura!'

'Mrs Byrne and I. . . .'

'Thank you,' I said, and pushed past him out of the room.

I can see still the star of bright sky; see the sun on the cutting edges of the glass.

I live with voices, touches, the violations of the past.

I am afraid now of the dark, because in the dark there seems to be no escape from those voices; the breathing, the hands winding, binding my hair tight around my neck, the gentle sound of the door handle turning, the humiliation of helplessness.

I sleep with a night light in my room, like a child. I never did that as a child; then I liked the dark, I liked the patterns of moon, clouds, play of light and shade on the walls and ceiling of my room. There was nothing then to frighten me, only the loved room, breathing around me. Now I keep a small bulb, hidden in a china house; the light from its windows and doors breaks welcomingly into the darkness for me.

Maurice thinks this is foolishness.

He likes velvet blackness, curtains tight shut, no cracks or glimmers of light to surprise his eyes.

'Like the womb, dote,' he said, more than once. 'Black like the womb, that's the way I think it ought to be.'

'I think I should go.'

Dominic's voice startled her.

The room was almost dark now; and outside the only light came from a crack between the hill and the sky.

'I'm sorry. . . . Oh, I am sorry. Do you have to? Do you want to?'

He didn't answer.

'Turn on the light.'

'I like it like this.' But nonetheless he got up and went over to the door and pressed the switch.

They blinked at each other as light filled the room and their eyes.

She banged with her fingers on the table for a moment, rhythmically.

Thumb, one, two. Thumb, one, two.

'I shouldn't have married Maurice.'

'Why do you say that?'

'We . . . ell . . . I'm not really superb wife material. I have none of the right instincts. I didn't need to get married for my own sake. . . . I wanted a child. I wanted to secure my line. Keep this house in the family.'

She smiled for a second. 'I was prepared to sacrifice freedom for that. . . . Maurice and I don't hate each other or anything like that, in fact we get on quite well. I could have run that mill you know, just as well as he does. That sounds like boasting, but it's true. I see now that I should have lived here alone and become an old battleaxe.'

He just stood inside the door and stared at her.

'You are the most beautiful woman I have ever seen.'

'Yes,' she said. 'A beautiful old battleaxe. That Protestant bitch above in her big house, who does she think she is, anyway?'

'People don't say things like that nowadays.'

'No?'

'I never hear people say things like that.'

'People are quite careful who they say that sort of thing to.'

'Probably.'

'Maurice tells me what they say. His family and their friends. Insidious, hurtful jokes. He thinks I should be amused. I laugh, of course. Yes. Not much point in doing anything else. Is there?'

He shook his head. 'Paranoia. . . .'

She laughed. 'There are lots of labels you could hang on me. I go through the label list regularly myself. There isn't one I haven't tried for size.'

She rattled her fingers on the table again and then got up. She began to clear the cups and plates from the table.

He never moved.

She touched the radio button and the building crescendos of *Carmina Burana* began to fill the room. She switched the sound off after a moment.

'I hate that music.'

'Why?'

'I don't know. It's creepy. Dangerous.'

'I wouldn't know. I don't listen much to music. I don't have the privacy. My head is so full of all the noises of the school all day long, all evening long, that when I shut the door of my room at night, I just like to hear silence. I don't even have a radio.'

She opened the dishwasher and put the cups and saucers in. Her hair hung down her back, thick and straight. She looked like a young girl, her face pale in spite of the wind and sun that she liked to live with, and her bones small, almost as if she were not yet fully grown.

He stared at her in silence as she moved here and there, ordering the room.

'I think I'll be off,' he said.

She looked round, surprised. 'I had it in my head you'd be staying to supper. I have enough food.'

He shook his head.

'No . . . I think . . . they'll be expecting me. I never said . . . they'll be expecting. . . .'

'Suit yourself.'

'Yes. Thanks for the tea.'

He turned and went out of the room. He walked quickly through the dark hall and opened the door. It was cold outside; a little wind was starting to stir the branches. He almost slammed the door behind him and ran down the avenue towards the lights that lit the main road into the town. Laura stood by the sink in the kitchen and listened to him leaving.

'Oh, bugger everything,' she said.

The next morning she put on her tidy clothes and went to church.

IN LOVING MEMORY OF HARRIET O'MEARA, LOST AT SEA.

Lost.

A shining brass plaque let into the wall just up above her pew.

Lost.

'A text?' the rector had asked. 'Do you want a text?'

She had shaken her head.

Father had wanted the works; texts, loving messages, dates, ornate plaited flowers, even angels.

'Just those words,' Laura had said.

Lost at sea.

Twenty-two people, also in their tidy clothes, made up the congregation. They stood and knelt and prayed and sang loudly so that their thin voices might penetrate out through the grey walls, be heard on the street outside; that was why she sang loudly, anyway.

I will not get lost.

Spare thou them, O God, which confess their faults.

Restore thou them that are penitent.

'It is forbidden,' Father had said.

'What is forbidden?'

'You know well it is forbidden for us to participate. . . .'

'I never realised, Father, that you would allow yourself to be bullied.'

He went red in the face and didn't speak.

'To look for a minute or two at a brass plaque

commemorating your wife. . . . What is that partici-
pating *in*? What secret, depraved ceremony could
currupt you? Tell me that. Do you really believe
yourself to be uncorrupted? Or perhaps you're
afraid that people will stop voting for you if they
see you going into that pathetic little Protestant
church?'

'God, but you've turned into a proper little bitch.
I should never have let you go skiving off to France
like that.'

*We praise Thee O God, we acknowledge Thee to be the
Lord.*

All the earth doth worship Thee, the Father everlasting.

*To Thee all angels cry aloud, the heavens and all the
powers therein.*

It was two years to the day – the day they spread
the spinnaker on the grass in front of the house.

The chestnut trees were again turning orange.

There was no dog to whine or bark.

They stood, Laura and her father, side by side in
the church.

She wore a black coat and her hair was still short
like a boy's hair and he stood beside her, hat in
hand, and stared inimicably at his shoes. The
chauffeur-driven Mercedes, his symbol of rank,
stood outside the gate, the engine running so that
he could make a quick getaway.

Mr Burroughs, the rector, stood with his back to
the altar, welcoming them with his hands.

The church was cold.

The church was always cold.

Laura gestured towards the plaque.

'Father.'

He raised his head and cleared his throat. The
sound of it ripped round the church.

'There's not much to it,' he said.

'We could of course have had something much

more elaborate,' said the rector apologetically, 'but. . . .'

'That's the way she would have liked it,' said Laura.

The rector gave a little cough.

'Quite,' he said.

O go your way into his gates with thanksgiving and into his courts with praise:

Be thankful unto him and speak good of his name.

For the Lord is gracious, his mercy is everlasting: and his truth endureth from generation to generation.

Mr Burroughs then moved towards them, smiling.

'Yes,' said Father. 'Well, I've seen it now. Very nice. Very. I. . . .' He cleared his throat again. '. . . must be on my way. Thank you, reverend . . . thank you. . . . Duty calls. Yes.'

He turned abruptly and clattered up the length of the aisle as if demons were at his heels.

The grace of our Lord Jesus Christ, the love of God. . . .

Lost.

And the fellowship of the Holy Ghost. . . .

In loving memory.

. . . be with you and remain with you all evermore.

In loving memory.

Amen.

Dominic was standing by the end of the lane that led up to the back of the school. He was wearing jeans and a sweat shirt. He watched her as she walked along the path and when she came abreast of him he joined her.

'I've the day off. One Sunday in four I'm on duty. I thought you might like a hand with the heavy work. Or maybe you don't. . . .'

'Oh, I do. I have never kept the Sabbath for reading holy books. I wasn't going to have any lunch . . . just a cup of coffee and then get stuck in.'

'That's O.K. by me.'

'Well . . . thank you. I won't say no.'

'I'm sorry about last night. I just suddenly remembered I had said I'd take Mick Hurley's duty. He's engaged. His fiancée hates him doing Saturday evening duty. He'd have had my life if I'd let him down. You know the way these things are?'

'Yes.'

'I didn't know whether you went to church or not.'

'If I go, I only go when Maurice is away.'

'How odd.'

'It irks him to watch me going in there. I can see the irritation in his face. He doesn't have much time for failures and I think he reckons the Church of Ireland to be some sort of pathetic failure. He doesn't spend many weekends at home.'

They walked for a moment in silence. Two fine chestnut trees by the avenue gate were bursting into bud.

'He sees a lot of people. Does business all the time, even when he seems to be relaxing. He's orderly, likes things to be utterly within his command. That's why I wondered if you might be a priest.'

'Why?'

'When you first came, I just wondered. My father had a habit of bringing young, handsome priests home. He sort of left them lying around in the hopes that my mother . . . that they . . . well, you know the way these things can happen. He always, always hoped that she would turn and of course bring me with her. He really believed in the One True Religion. She was much too clever a fish to snap at that bait. They loved her and kept coming back, for her company and her cooking . . . a couple of them even went sailing with her. I thought perhaps that Maurice was up to the same trick. He doesn't really have much imagination.'

'So you thought I was a handsome young priest.'

She blushed and laughed and said nothing.

'And instead I am a recusant. I think that's the right word for someone who defies the authority of the Church.'

'No one uses that word any more.'

'Recusant?'

'So many words aren't used now. They are becoming lost to us. I worry sometimes about all those lost words. It becomes more and more difficult to make yourself understood without them . . . and when you do use them people think you're batty. It's best to keep quiet. I keep quiet.'

The gravel crunched beneath their feet and the smell of drifting turf smoke was in the air.

'I haven't noticed. It seems to me you talk the hind leg off a donkey.'

She laughed. 'I'm sorry.'

'I like it. Maybe I'm a donkey.'

They had reached the bottom of the shallow steps that led up to the front door. Again he heard the distant sound of music coming from the house. She looked at him with a little smile, about to say something, and then in the distance a dog barked. The smile disappeared and she stood quite still for a moment, her head slightly to one side, listening to the sound.

She ran up the steps and opened the hall door.

'I'll be with you in a second,' she said to him over her shoulder and was gone again away from him.

I see her again.
Running.
Showing a clean pair of heels; I've always loved that daft expression.
In black, as usual.
Always black.
She could be any age.
My age.
My mother's age.
My daughter's age.
If I had a daughter.
Through the opening trees.
She leaves no mark on the grass as she runs. Her dress flutters and flows, streaming from her sides like water.
All ages.
All women.
Fifteen is a bad age.
Little pet. My beautiful little pet. Isn't she a little beauty? Growing up. Yes. Growing up to be a lady, like her mammy. A real lady. A queen.
There is nowhere to run.
I want to shout that to her out of the window.
Nowhere.
No one.
But I can never move when I see her, never speak the words that I want to speak.
Tell me where? She might call that to me one day.
No where.
My queen.
My hair used to spark and crackle when I brushed it.

Just a little kiss for Daddy.

Fingers on my neck, under my hair, tightening fingers, thumb stroking, circling on the blade bone of my shoulder.

'Laura!'

The rhododendrons are flowering now along that path, under the tall trees, red, pink, huge white cabbage blooms, crimson, scarlet, flame.

Brilliant forerunners of summer.

Campylocarpum, Falconeri, Augustinii, Cornish Cross. Mother knew them all. Cinnebarinum roylei. Every name, every plant, like people she knew them, their habits, their foibles.

'Laura. Are you all right?'

It is not my father, nor is it Maurice.

Outside the window the world is empty. The heavy rhododendron flowers and the half-opened leaves on the chestnut trees stir.

Dominic is standing in the doorway of the room, afraid, it seems, to come in.

'Yes. Yes, of course I'm all right. Just mooning. My mother always said that about me. Mooning. That was one of her great words. Forgive me.'

'I made some coffee. I was dying for a cup of coffee, so I rustled around in your kitchen and. . . .'

'I can come now. I will come now.'

'Laura. Come quick. Look. Come here. Come and see.'

His voice was full of excitement.

For a couple of hours he had been attacking a huge thicket of bamboo; slashing, pulling, chopping, and ineffectually digging at the roots with a spade. Now he had come across what seemed to be the corner of a stone step.

'Laura!'

She dragged some branches out from the under-growth and threw them on the fire and then came towards him.

'What's up?'

'I think I've found it. I think . . . look here . . . a step. Yes? Or maybe it's just a large stone . . . but I think. . . .'

She scrambled over the cut bamboo and squatted down beside him. She pulled off a glove and put her hand on the stone; then she turned and smiled up at him, her face filled with delight. Without a word they cut and tugged at the bamboo and the tangled weeds until the whole step, about three feet long, was uncovered.

It was a granite step, with tiny sparks of mica shining in the discovering sunlight.

She sat down on it and put her two hands over her face; he thought for a moment that perhaps she was praying, but she was looking for her mother's face in the darkness and privacy of her cupped hands. There was no face there to be seen, no sign. There never was. She had to look at her portrait in the dining room, at posed formal photographs, in the books of snapshots, to remember how she had really looked.

Dominic leant towards her and brushed away some twigs that had caught in her hair.

She took her hands from her face and looked up at him, startled by the touch.

'It was just . . .' His voice was apologetic . . . 'just twigs in. . . .'

'Dominic. . . .'

'. . . your hair.'

'Laura!'

They were both puzzled for a moment by the call.

'He's home.'

She stood up.

'Maurice. I didn't expect him for ages yet. We'd better. . . .'

'Laura!'

'Coming.' She whispered the word, and gathering up the sickle and the clippers and a spade, she began to walk towards the house.

He was standing outside the front door, jingling the coins in his pocket impatiently.

Two cars were parked in the drive below the house.

Oh, God, she thought, as she walked up through the fields. He's brought people back with him.

Maurice didn't move. He didn't wave or anything like that, just stood there jingling, turning the coins over and over and then from time to time shaking them in his impatient hand.

As she crossed the gravel, he spoke.

'Where have you been? I've brought the Poulencs for tea. God, you look a sight!'

'I didn't expect you so early. Not for tea. Actually, I didn't think you'd be back till all hours.'

'What on earth have you been doing? If you could see yourself!'

She dumped the tools at the top of the steps.

'And who's that?' He nodded towards Dominic who was trailing up the field slowly.

'Dominic. We've been gardening.'

'Dominic?'

'O'Hara.'

'Oh, him.'

He put a hand on her shoulder and turned her towards the house; a quick push and she was in the hall. She moved away from him and stooped to take off her boots.

'We've been clearing down near the river . . . you know, where I. . . .'

'Go on up and change, Laura. Sandra's keeping the Poulencs entertained. We'll be in your sitting room when you're ready.'

She stood up, her eyes a little dizzy from rushing up through the fields and from stooping down.

'In. . . .'

'I lit the fire. Don't be long.'

He walked across the hall and up the stairs.

She went into the cloakroom and turned on the taps.

'Fuck,' she said to herself in the glass. 'Fuck, fuck, fuck.' Her face was smeared with smoke and mud.

'I look like some sort of Red Indian,' she said as Dominic came into the room. 'Covered in war paint or camouflage.'

They stared at themselves in the glass.

'You're just as bad.'

'We're a couple of swells,' he began to sing. 'We stay at the best hotels. . . .'

'Wash.'

'Dedadadadedada, far from the city smells.'

She bent and splashed water over her face.

'Wash, Dominic.'

'The Vanderbilts have asked us out to tea. . . .'

'You must wash and come and protect me from the French. They're upstairs expecting cake and *politesse*.'

'No. I'm going back to have toasted, sliced pan loaf and correct Latin texts.'

'Well, wash first, in case you meet someone you know on the way home.'

'I'm not bothered. It's what my mother used

to call clean dirt. I'm so glad we've found your summerhouse.'

She nodded.

'Yes. I was afraid. . . . Yes. Yes. I'm glad too. Very glad.'

Water ran down her neck and under her shirt, splattered onto the floor.

'Will you come back?'

'Soon.'

Trays, cups, saucers, plates, spoons, a knife, cake, sugar, milk, teapot, hot-water jug.

Mother would have had sandwiches, the bread cut so thin that it was almost transparent, and scones straight from the oven, with curls of butter and homemade jam. Teresa or Bridie or Katie or Nellie, dressed in their black afternoon dresses, would have seen to things.

Water spluttered out of the spout of the kettle and the lid rattled.

'Mummy, I want to go to boarding school.'

'Not now, dear. Bring that tray into the drawing room for me. That awful Senator Quinlan has arrived to see your father, and his wife and a son. They all need tea. And it's Thursday.'

Thursday was Nellie or Bridie or Katie's day off.

'I do want to go to boarding school. . . .'

'Then change out of those ghastly clothes. Get a move on, Laura . . . we'll talk about it later.'

That was Maurice, she thought . . . he must have been eighteen or nineteen, bored out of his mind, allowed to drive the old Daimler for the first time; she remembered that, remembered his bored silence. There's no such thing as a free lunch.

She tilted some boiling water into the teapot and swirled it round.

A clatter of high heels.

She threw the water into the sink.

'Can I help?'

Sandra stood in the doorway.

'Well, I. . . .'

'Maurice insisted we came. You must see the place in daylight, he said. I'm sorry. I thought, what a bore for Laura. No warning. Ring. I said to him, ring, but he said you'd be delighted. Men can be so thoughtless.'

'I'm delighted,' said Laura. Indian or China, she pondered in her mind.

'It was a gorgeous drive. I love the spring. You're probably used to all this freshness, like, living in the country. All the trees and that. Flowers, gorgeous colour. You're so lucky to live in the country.'

China, she decided.

'You should have come up with Maurice. The O'Briens were so kind. . . . The way they live is fabulous. Nothing stinted, you know. Nothing. They think the world of Maurice. Of course, you know that. You should have. . . . I like racing, don't you? I made twenty-five quid. Fabulous.'

One, two, three, four spoonfuls.

'You don't go places, do you?'

'Not very often.'

'Beginner's luck, they all said. I just chose by the name, you know. I always do that. I pick a name I like and wham, that's the one I put the cash on. Not what you'd call scientific. Mind you, twenty-five quid was nothing to them. Sundance . . . one of them was . . . I had to choose that . . . you know, Butch Cassidy and. . . .'

'You carry the tray, would you? And I'll be up after you with the tea. Thanks a lot.'

'Chocky cake, how gorgeous. Maurice says you make lovely cakes and never eat them.'

She picked up the loaded tray and headed for the door.

'I hope I don't drop it. I'm sure those cups and saucers are precious. Maurice says you have a fabulous lot of precious things.'

Laura poured the boiling water onto the tea. The scented smell curled up into her nose.

Sandra's hand waved out of the back window of the car.

Mme Poulenc inclined her head graciously.

M.Poulenc's hand gripped tight to the steering wheel; he sported two gold rings and highly polished nails.

It was raining.

Just what they expected.

En Irlande il pleut toujours.

Maurice and Laura stood on the steps and watched until the car was round the corner.

Maurice's arm lay lightly across her shoulders.

Weightless.

Il pleure dans mon coeur comme il pleut sur la ville. Who wrote that?

The car horn bleated as M.Poulenc turned out of the gate.

'I hope they get safely back to Dublin. His driving is a little volatile.'

He gave her shoulder a little squeeze before removing his arm.

'Poor Sandra'll be in bits by the end of the journey. She offered to drive back but he wouldn't let her. I hope you didn't mind, dote.'

They turned and went into the house.

One thing about the rain at this time of year, it wasn't cold. Just warm water gently falling from the sky.

'No. Of course I didn't mind.'

'You should have tidied up a bit.'

'I don't suppose they cared.'

'I. . . .'

'Oh, you. . . .'

'. . . like them to see you at your best.'

She laughed. 'I don't suppose it will affect the sales of animal foodstuffs in Europe.'

He looked cross but didn't say anything.

'You could run up and bring me down the tea things, if you want to be really helpful, and I'll. . . .'

'I have some telephoning to do. What was the schoolmaster doing here, anyway? He's a dull sod.'

'I thought he was a friend of yours.'

'Not at all. I'm just interested in promoting the school team. I hoped that he and O'Brien might click . . . you know, get something moving. . . . They say he's a spoiled priest.'

'Do they?'

'He has that look about him . . . a bit sour. Know what I mean?'

He turned back towards the door. 'I'll be down in the office if you want me. Shouldn't be too long. Let's have something light for supper. I don't seem to have stopped eating all weekend.'

It rained then for four days without ceasing.

Streams and rivers became turbulent and low-lying fields were spread with unwelcome lakes and ponds.

Grey clouds seemed only a hand's stretch from the rooftops.

Everywhere there was the sound of water, running, splashing, dripping, sighing, crying.

'Fucking weather.'

Maurice came into her room, buzzing at his face with his cordless razor.

Father stroked the long leather strop with the razor blade, his fingers gently curled around the bone handle. His testing thumb moved for a moment to the cutting edge, and then the hissing of the blade on the leather started again. When the blade pleased his thumb, he nodded, and she held up the bowl of soap for him, like an acolyte. Bright brass taps; steam curled from the basin. Carefully he lathered and stroked his face with the blade, wiped the soap from the blade onto a folded white towel, rinsed, smoothed, patted, stroked, dried. Then his eyes turned from the glass down towards her. He took the bowl from her hands and set it by the basin and, bending down, gently he took her hand in his.

'Feel,' he said. 'Feel that, now. . . .' He touched her fingers to his chest, his throat, his chin.

'Smooth as a baby's bottom. Yes?'

'Yes,' she whispered.

Then he put his arms around her, pulled her face against his warm bare stomach, and held her. Below somewhere, a voice called, or maybe it was the sound of the breakfast gong, she couldn't recall. His arms relaxed. His hand gave her a little push towards the door.

'Run along, pet. My little helper.'

She was standing, head bent down, brushing her hair.

A hundred strokes she gave it, morning and evening. Good for the circulation of blood round the head, if nothing else. Bending down and brushing, leaning back and brushing, and in the winter the crackle of static running the length of her hair with each stroke of the brush.

As she straightened up her hair flew round her and then settled like a cape over her shoulders.

He waved the razor at her and felt his left cheek with his fingers.

'I'm for town. I've a meeting with the Minister at eleven, then we're giving the Poulencs lunch and putting . . . well, probably pouring them onto the plane.'

He buzzed the razor again round the line of his jaw. 'Don't fuss about food. I'm not sure what time I'll be back.'

He dropped the razor into his dressing gown pocket and came over to her.

'Pity about the rain. Old Poulenc has taken Ireland to his boooosom. He's not too keen on the old *pluie*, though.' He put his hand under her hair onto the back of her neck and his fingers stroked her for a moment.

'You O.K., dote? It's rotten weather for gardening. Anything you want in town?'

He removed his hand and looked at himself in the mirror.

'No thanks. Nothing.'

'Do you think I'm putting on weight?'

He touched his jaw with his fingers.

'Jowls, I mean. I hate jowls.'

'Not a jowl in sight,' she said reassuringly.

He bent and kissed her cheek.

'Lovely lady.'

'What do you mean, you want to go to boarding school?' Mother came into the sitting room and closed the door behind her.

'Thank God those awful people have gone.'

She walked to the window and pulled over the curtains, pressing them close together to keep out the wind and the rain.

'I think Daddy's going to bring that boy into the mill . . . so, we're all going to have to be palsy walsy. At least he . . . what'shisname . . . seems to know how to keep his mouth shut.'

She sat down on the opposite side of the fire to me.

'For the time being, anyway. Well?'

'I just do. I want to go.'

'Why? Laura, you must have some notion why. It can't be just a whim, you know.'

'Well. . . .'

I had worked out just what I was going to say to her, but the words seemed to have abandoned me.

'Well?'

'Well? Well, what?' Her voice was impatient.

'I hate it there. They're horrid to me. They won't play with me. They never ask me to play or anything. They call me names.'

'It's only your first term, for heaven's sake. You'll settle. I'll have a word with. . . .'

'No, please, Mummy, don't have a word with anyone. . . . They call me Proddy bitch and West Brit. I hate it. I don't want to settle. . . . I want to go to boarding school.'

'Who calls you these things?'

I shook my head.

'That's all rubbish and you know it. All children tease each other. They'll settle. You'll settle. You'll see. In a year you'll all be terrific pals and you'll be laughing about this.'

'You've never had people say things like that to you. You don't know what it's like.'

'Fight,' said Mother.

'How can I fight? Tell me how. What can I say

back to them? What do you want me to do . . . set them on fire?'

'Don't be silly, Laura. Sometimes you can be so silly.'

'Black their eyes? Break their arms?'

'Laura!'

'They hid all my books yesterday . . . just cleared everything out of my desk. I hadn't a single book for any class. I have to stay in every afternoon next week.'

'Why didn't you tell the teachers? I'll go and see Reverend Mother on. . . .'

'No. You know what they'll call me if you do that? Tell tale tit, your tongue shall be slit. Informer. You know about informers.'

'You are being overemotional.' She plaited her fingers together and looked at me over the tops of them. 'You have been overprotected,' she said after a long silence.

'I want to go to boarding school.'

'Who are these girls?'

'I'm not telling you. There's quite a crowd of them . . . and all the rest just look on and laugh.'

'I'll talk to your father.'

'I don't want Daddy mixed up in this. I don't want him running off to the school. I know he won't let me go. I know, I know. I don't want him saying no. I don't want to stay here. I can't stay here. Mummy, please believe me.'

I began to cry and I couldn't see her anymore through my tears. He won't let me go. He won't let me go. He won't let me go. Mother couldn't hear those words, but they beat in my head, they beat the tears out of my eyes. Tears flooded down my cheeks.

Dominic came again of course, plodding up the avenue through the rain. She watched him out of the kitchen window and laughed at him as he came in the door.

'You must watch. You must spy,' she said to him, as she watched him shaking drops from his hair like a dog after a swim.

He blushed. 'I do have to say I saw him setting off this morning. Dublinwards. I thought I'd take a chance on his not being back this afternoon.'

'Do you not have work to do?'

'Are you not pleased to see me?'

They stood in silence for a moment while she considered what she should answer.

'Why don't you come when Maurice is here?'

'I don't like him. I see no harm in saying that. I hope you don't mind. He doesn't like me. I do like you. QED.' Rain splattered against the long window. 'In fact. . . .' he said.

'Let's go out and walk in the rain. Come on. Let's get really wet. I'll take you down and show you the remains of the little pier. Did you know we had a little pier?'

She rushed past him out of the room and across the hall, talking as she went. 'It's falling to bits now. Who needs a little pier these days? I was going to take a run down there anyway this afternoon. I love wet and stormy days. I'll have your company now. That will be nice.'

She pulled on her gumboots. 'O.K?'

He was standing beside her and he put out a hand and touched her bent head. She shook his hand off almost violently.

'Do not do that. I might fall apart. Please don't take me by surprise by doing that sort of thing.'

She straightened up.

'I'm sorry.

She opened the hall door and they went out into the rain.

'I'm sorry,' he repeated.

'I'm sorry,' he said, 'if I've done something to upset you.'

'No, you haven't. It's just sometimes . . . a hand on my head . . . will, makes me . . . gives me the creeps. I sometimes want to scream. That's all. Sorry. Nothing personal.'

She took his arm to show him there was nothing personal.

Half the little pier was down, granite blocks tumbling into the sea. The waves crashed against the remaining wall and spray flew up high towards the black sky. Gulls floated, lifted on the wind, sharp white, like the spray.

'You see how things fall apart,' she said.

They stood on the hill above the beach and stared down at the storm. The wind plucked and pulled at their clothes; the rain was relentless.

'My mother's grandfather built the pier. I think he thought that local fishermen could use it, but they never did. Actually there are no local fishermen. This stretch of the coast is too exposed.'

'Was that the travelling man?'

She nodded. 'Maybe he dreamed he might set off from here in his own boat, to bring back more bits and pieces . . . right back here, to his own pier. Home.'

She began to slither her way down through the bent grass and wet sand. He followed her.

'My mother made sure that everything was kept

up to the mark. Then when . . . after . . . well, my father didn't care about this place. He liked things to have their uses, and people too. "No use to me," he would say. And that was that. He let things fall apart; sometimes even people would never be seen again.'

Huge white rollers were pounding in towards them; spray as well as rain filled the air.

A crude flight of steps led up to the top of the pier; weed and green slime made each step treacherously slippy.

'Let's go up,' she said, and stepped up onto the first slab of stone.

'It looks dangerous.'

'Mmm. It is. Exciting. Mother never let me up here when there was a wind.'

She scrambled on up. A wave hit the outside of the pier and water crashed across the wall, spilling down on her as she climbed.

'Laura.'

'Come on.'

'Don't be damn stupid. I'm not going up there.'

'No.' She stopped and turned carefully round, trying to keep her feet from sliding on the steps.

'No more am I.' She jumped down beside him.

'Sometimes I feel filled with bravado – the thought of death seems rather magnificent. Then, phhhtt . . . I get stricken with fear again. Let's get away from here. I'm frozen. Let's run.'

'I'm not running. I'm too old to run. You run if you want to. I will walk sedately after you.'

'You're not old. What about all that rugby?'

'I'm too old for running uphill in wellington boots.'

They both walked in sedate silence until they reached the top of the hill, when they turned and looked once more down at the cove and the pier and the roaring sea.

'Was it from here your mother . . . ?'

She held out both arms towards the sea for a moment and then dropped them down once more by her sides.

'No shelter,' she said. 'You can see that for yourself. Dangerous coastline. Rocks, squalls, a very unkind coastline. But she knew, she understood that. I think if she'd been born a man, she would have spent her life sailing away somewhere, like her grandfather, always coming back here, perching for a moment, then off again. . . . Always bringing back presents for the people she loved, or objects of remembrance, filling the tiny space here with acknowledgments that there is a world out there.'

She stood for a moment, her head bent as if trying to catch the voices in the wind.

'I think she hated being a woman. I think she hated having to turn over her independence to someone else. She escaped inside her head, and of course in her boat. She used to spend so much time scudding round those headlands. I'm sure she had such dreams in her head. I'd love to have known what they were. She never revealed anything. Each evening the dog and I would. . . .'

She nodded her head towards the pier.

'. . . wait.'

'What was the dog's name?'

She looked at him for a moment before replying.

'I don't remember.'

Pekoe. Pekoe. Pekoe.

'We'll call him Pekoe.'

'Why?' asked Daddy.

'Because he's orange . . . I suppose we could call him King Billy, but I prefer Pekoe.'

Pekoe.
Pekoe.
Why can't I speak your name?

I am not sure in which tense I live, the present or the past.

Both seem irreconcilably intermingled in my mind.

The future doesn't bother me.

The future has no reality for me.

Anything could happen.

Nothing could happen.

It's all the same to me.

I get up each morning because I have always got up each morning and I see no reason to change my ways.

Maybe it was twenty years ago that she sailed on the blue turbulent sea and the gulls reflected the straining sails; or maybe it was yesterday.

No.

Yesterday it was raining. I know that much. It rained yesterday as it is raining now, streaming, grey rain, and the gulls are grey and they cry as they hover just over the waves, scanning the sea for food.

'You keep going away.'

His voice made her jump.

'Sorry.'

'That's all right, but sometimes you look as if you might never come back, as if you might stay permanently in that land inside your head.'

'Aren't we daft? We should have stayed indoors,

lit a huge fire, listened to Bach, Schubert, Mozart, drank cups of tea, told each other stories. . . .'

'Stop.'

'. . . kept the devils at bay.'

'What devils?'

They walked along the track through the whin bushes, back towards the town. Sheep, their fleece weighted down with water, huddled under the trees.

'Just any old devils that happen to be passing.'

He took hold of her hand; she didn't seem to notice.

'Will you ever get married, do you think?'

'I don't see it. I find the notion of that sort of commitment very hard to take on board. Like your mother I think I want to go where the wind and waves take me. I've never been troubled by women. I don't mean I'm. . . .' He looked rather anxiously towards her.

She nodded her head but didn't speak.

'I've often wondered if God is punishing me for not being able to love him enough, serve him, celebrate him as I was trained to do . . . as, I must say I would have liked to do. Maybe I will roam through life without either giving or receiving love. That is a fierce punishment.'

'You must have loved your parents. Everyone, one way or another. . . .'

'I was impaled on the spike of their ambitions for me, right from the word go. I found that painful always, and not very love-inspiring. . . . I have been sorry for them. I also have to say that I have hated them. Yes.'

His grip on her fingers was quite painful, but she didn't dare wriggle her hand free.

'"Is there a woman at the back of this?" Those

were the words my father shouted at me the morning I went to confirm, in person, that I had left. I was flabbergasted . . . almost knocked off my feet by the sound of his voice. He has this big desk in his room and he was sitting behind it with my letter in his hand, just waiting for me to come in through the door. At least, that's what it seemed like to me. I suppose I didn't choose my time very well. But, I couldn't . . . Laura . . . I was truly released by her death . . . I couldn't wait another day. He threw my letter down on top of a pile of papers with such contempt . . . Yes, contempt. "Is there a woman at the back of this?"'

He let go of her hand and rubbed for a moment at his face.

'"Of course there isn't a woman anywhere. I have left, Father. . . ." He banged on the table with his fist . . . like a child having a tantrum. I was actually frightened for a moment. The papers in front of him rustled and scattered, falling on the floor, some of them, and I didn't know whether to bend down and pick them up or leave them. "I am glad," he said. "I am truly glad that your mother isn't alive on this shameful day." He picked up his pen and began to write something on a piece of paper. He didn't speak. I stood there looking down at him. I didn't know whether to go or stay. There was an old clock on the mantlepiece and I could hear its tick-tock, tick-tock, and the sound of his pen scratching on the paper.'

'People can be very insensitive.'

There really was no need for her to say anything stupid like that.

He groped for her hand again and held it close to his side. 'He never uses a ball point. He has this black and gold fountain pen. He's had it ever since I can remember. I haven't seen him since. He won't even speak to me on the telephone. I suppose it doesn't really matter. I suppose . . . I suppose. . . . Anyway, it's my sisters now won't let me near him. He's ill, you know. Cooped up in bed. . . . I think very ill. I think . . . they protect him from the likes of me . . . from botherment.'

They had reached the main road. He let go of her hand and looked morosely at the ground.

'Barge in,' she said. 'Don't let them stop you. Just. . . .' She waved her arms in the air. 'Knock them down if need be. Fight.' The word echoed in her head.

He laughed. 'My sisters are pillars of the community. It's quite hard to knock down a pillar of the community.'

'Nonetheless.'

'You're soaking. Drowned.'

He was annoyed by his use of that word, but she wasn't listening to him.

'Is he . . . your father . . . is he dying?'

'So they say. I speak to one or other of them each day. They unwillingly give me information. He's eighty-six. He just lies there, they say. They don't want him upset. They don't want things brought into his mind that might . . . well . . . you know.'

Forgive me, he had said.

I had to stoop towards him to catch the words, so frail was his voice.

Will you?

I put my hand on his: for a moment his fingers were still; then as I lifted my hand, the restless tearing and plucking began again.

'Just barge in. Don't tell anyone you're coming, just barge. I am the son. Say that to them. They know nothing . . . those sisters. You see, we need to know how to forgive as well as to be forgiven.'

He nodded, and turning away without a word, he walked down the road towards the school.

'Fight,' she called after him.

Maurice came the next afternoon to find out what she was doing down near the stream.

The rain had stopped and the sun seemed to be sucking the water up from the land, and with it the springing grass and the uncurling leaves. The stream, full after all the rain, splashed and sang through the undergrowth.

'Imagine that, now,' he said.

She had uncovered by then three steps and part of a low stone wall.

She straightened up slowly, her back muscles aching, and smiled at him.

'Do you remember it?'

'How could I, for heaven's sake.'

'Try. Think back.'

'But you said yourself it was gone before I came here.'

'Do you remember the first time we met?'

'Vividly. Trinity Ball, 1971 . . . you. . . .'

'No. No. Think back . . . way before that.'

'. . . wiped the floor with all the other girls. Demolished them.'

'Years before that.'

'I never. . . .'

'Yes. I suddenly remembered the other day. You came down to tea with your mother and father. . . . I must have been about. . . .'

'I don't remember. Never saw you before in my life until. . . .'

'. . . thirteen. They sent us out for a walk because. . . .'

'. . . that night. Where have you been all my life? Didn't I say that to you?'

'. . . they wanted to talk business. . . .'

'Didn't I?'

'. . . business arrangements. You must have known what they were. . . . You seemed very grown up to me.'

'Where have you been all my life?'

'I couldn't think of a thing to say. I was totally silenced by shyness and your grownupness. We sat on these steps and you smoked a cigarette and swanked about driving the Daimler down from Dublin.'

'The Daimler?'

'Yes.'

'I remember that old car. God, that was umpteen years ago. Are you sure?'

She nodded.

'She was a lovely car to drive. Mother sold her when Dad died. For a bloody song, as you can imagine. That car would be worth a fortune now. We must be getting old. That must have been twenty-five years ago.'

'We sat on these steps.'

'Strange, I don't remember a thing.'

'It used to be painted pink.'

'What?'

She laughed.

'The summerhouse . . . a sort of dusty Italian pink.'

'I'll send one of the men down with a digger. . . .'

'No. No, thanks. Don't do that. I want to discover it myself. Little by little. Unfold it all.'

'Suit yourself.'

He shifted his feet, impatient suddenly, wanting to be somewhere else.

'That bonfire smoke is very bad for you, you know. Carcinogenic.'

'People have been making bonfires since man learnt to rub two sticks together.'

'That's not the point. . . .'

She started to scrape away again at the clinging ivy on the low wall.

'I reckon I'm as likely to die from cancer caused by the smoke from that bonfire as you are to die in a plane crash between here and the Caribbean.'

'Sometimes you can be quite unpleasant.'

He turned and walked away.

'Sorry,' she called after him.

His feet squelched on the wet grass.

I have always slept with my bedroom windows open, one in the winter and both of them in the summer.

Maurice thinks I am crazy.

It is one of the reasons he gave me for moving into another bedroom.

'Ruination of the tubes, dote,' he said. 'I want my tubes intact to the bitter end.'

He likes the windows closed and the curtains pulled tight, no chink or hint of light – no night light in a china house – to disturb his rest.

Though I feel constantly troubled by the dangers of indoor darkness, I do still like to hear the dawn chorus and the distant sound of the sea.

They haven't changed much down the years, the sounds that always signalled safety to me: the breathing of the earth, the sharp bark of a fox in the night; and the owl, whose mournful cry used to scare me when I was a child, now gives me peace.

How long do owls live? I could swear that this is the same voice that screeches in the night.

This owl is thirty if it is a day.

Neither are trees silent; the branches, stirred by the wind, rub together, sometimes creak and groan as if burdened by too great a weight of leaves. Leaves whisper amongst themselves.

Badgers, rats, foxes, mice, shrews, weasels, owls, bats, moths, all fill the summer nights with their comings and goings. And, of course, the sea; the crescendos and diminuendos of advance, retreat, sigh, forever sighing, laughing, crying, winning, losing; my cradle-to-the-grave song.

Day by day the summerhouse was stripped of its protection.

She worked alone, grubbing out, cutting, chopping, sometimes not looking up for an hour at a time from the tangled weeds and scrub to see the effects of her clearing.

Three stone steps led up to a stone balcony and a moss-covered balustrade. Under a neat pillared archway the door hung, half devoured by time and damp. The glass panes in the windows were broken and the window frames rotted; the smell of damp stone and rotting wood was faintly sickening to her as it drifted from the house. A weeping willow with a crooked trunk leaned away from the summerhouse, its whippy branches now bursting into leaf, and she could see the huge white flowers of a Falconeri growing up through the tangle above the roof.

'Cabbages,' Mother had said.

'I think they're lovely.'

'It just depends whether you like cabbages or not.'

'I like cabbages,' she said aloud then, looking up at the flowers, glad that they had survived, glad that she had remembered them and had heard at the moment of seeing the first cabbagelike flower, that stab of her mother's voice.

'Your father says no.'

Those had been the words that followed.

The weeping willow had been quite small then, only about eight feet high if she remembered aright.

Saileach is the Irish for willow.

Down by the Sally gardens, my love and I. . . .

'Why did he say no?'

Mother shrugged.

. . . did meet. She passed the. . . .

'Why?'

. . . Sally Gardens with. . . .

'Darling, he just said no. He said it in one of his positive voices.'

Saileach is the Irish for willow.

'You didn't argue? You didn't . . . ? I know why he said no.'

Treading on dangerous ground there, Laura. I clamped my mouth shut.

'Don't let's have a row about it, Laura.' Mother's voice rose sharply. 'I think you'll get used to it. . . . It's so much nicer for you to be at home. . . . It's really a very good school, you know . . . you will get used to it. You'll forget about all this nonsense. You've got to get used to it Laura, and neither your father nor I want to hear any more about it from you.'

The world split into fragments as the tears burst from my eyes.

Mother didn't look up from her gardening. I could hear the sound of the trowel sliding into the earth.

I ran.

When I got to the house, I ran along the terrace, past the windows of the sitting room and in the back door. I could see nothing, only the dazzling of my tears.

He was outside my bedroom door. Between me and the door, there was the warm rock of his body.

He caught me in his arms and held me tight against him.

'Little pet,' he murmured.

I couldn't fight.

I was drowning in my tears and in the warmth of his body.

He put his hand under my chin and turned my face up towards his.

I shut my eyes tight so that I wouldn't have to see his face.

'It will be all right. You must believe me, Laura. I know what is best for us all. Everything will be all right.'

I felt his tongue on the right side of my face, lapping like a cat at the tears.

From my chin to the bone beneath the socket of my eye I felt the browsing of his thirsty tongue.

I punched him in the stomach with my fist and pushed past him through the door into my room. I slammed the door behind me and shoved the armchair against it, though I knew that at that moment he wouldn't follow me in.

'Are you crying?'

She looked up from the past to see Dominic standing black between herself and the sun.

'No.'

She got up from the step and held her hand out to him. 'You're very welcome.'

'You have . . . there are tears on. . . .'

She shook her head violently, afraid for a moment that he might touch her face.

'Someone else was crying. A foolish . . . child. Look how much work I've done. Why should I cry? Look at all that. I've been flat out for days. I thought perhaps you had abandoned me.'

'I have been standing there for ages admiring it . . . watching you. . . . Admiring all that work. It's. . . .'

'Blow me, I said to myself . . . I've made him work too hard and he's. . . .'

'. . . wonderful. I never thought. . . .'

'. . . gone.'

'. . . it would be like this. Such a perfect little gem of a house.'

'And the cabbage tree. Please note. . . .'

'I went to see him. That's where I've been. I took a couple of days. I told them at the school that he was . . . I was able to shift some of my classes round.'

'Ah. Yes.'

'I took your. . . .'

She took a Kleenex out of her pocket and rubbed at her face and then blew her nose.

'Yes,' he said. 'I took your advice. I barged in.'

'You don't have to tell me about it if you don't want to.'

'There's not much to tell. Both my sisters were there . . . a bit unfortunate that. They behaved true to form. Lena raged at me and Detta cried. I felt a bloody heel. . . .'

'And your father?'

He shrugged.

'How can you tell? He just lay there. They

wouldn't leave me alone in the room with him. It wouldn't be right, Lena said. We always do what Lena says. They stood like warders, one on each side of me, and I just looked at him and he just looked upwards with his unfocused eyes. I don't know if he . . . I don't know.'

'It doesn't matter.'

'I wanted to stay. Just sit there, you know, beside him for a while. I didn't want to say anything . . . make any statements . . . nothing like that. Just sit. Sing, perhaps, like you sing to a baby. Comfortable songs.'

She put out a hand and touched his sleeve.

'They wouldn't let me. We don't want Papa upset. That's what she kept saying, said. We don't want. . . . And Detta cried.'

'That's nice,' she said. 'Papa. Old-fashioned. Nicer than Daddy, really. I think so.'

'We don't want him upset. . . . I'll go back.'

'Yes. You mustn't pay any attention to them.'

'Such a perfect little gem of a house.'

She smiled. 'A lot of work to do yet. I haven't dared open the door.'

'Let's. . . .' He took a step towards the summer-house but she stopped him.

'No. We'll wait until it's all cleared. Then. . . . It's probably full of dead rats and mouldering deck chairs.'

'A horrible smell.'

'Bats, worms, mice, spiders.'

'I hate spiders.'

'Rugs. I seem to remember rugs . . . and brightly coloured cushions.' Mother liked to be comfortable.

'Why were you crying?' He whispered the words.

'I was being pestered by an old ghost. Perhaps it's not a good thing to live all your life in one place. Hmn? What do you think?'

'It seems to me like a wonderful way of living. I have nowhere. I see myself moving from pillar to post, endlessly packing and unpacking my bags. I'm a wanderer rather than a traveller like your great-grandfather. He always knew why he was travelling. To come back here.'

She laughed. 'To father another child.'

'My bags will contain nothing. I will pack and unpack nothing, relentlessly.'

She began to gather up the tools that lay on the ground.

'You are depressed. Watching someone die. . . .' She handed him a fork. 'Here, carry this for me. I live the way I have chosen. People frighten me. Here I am protected from people. Causes frighten me. Here I am protected from causes. The future frightens me. Here I can pretend. . . .'

'Pretend what?'

She began to walk towards the house. He followed her, the fork jauntily over his shoulder.

They walked through a twist of smoke from the smouldering bonfire. For a moment his eyes stung and bubbled.

'Maybe my mother will sail around the corner in that little boat. The dog will bark. We will all begin again.'

Then she laughed. 'I'd hate that, really. I am so glad we only have one life.'

They walked in silence up through the field and through the gate that led into the walk under the rhododendrons. The grass was carpeted with petals, pink and white, like snow. The windows of the house were all open and the voice of Maria Callas spread out into the garden.

Divinités du Styx.

'Oh God, I love this so much.'

Divinités du Styx, ministres de la Mort.

'I'll make a cup of tea,' she said.

'You're always making cups of tea. Why? Why can't we just sit here on the grass and talk, or listen to the music?'

'I'm an addict. I like the ritual. I feel totally safe when I'm making cups of tea. I. . . .'

'Enough of that. Just sit down here, beside me. . . .'

The music stopped abruptly.

She stood quite still on the path, her head slightly tilted to one side, as if she could hear the singing inside her head.

'Dote.'

Maurice's voice.

The scraping of a chair on the tiles, footsteps.

'Laura. Is that you?'

He appeared at the back door.

'Dote. I just popped up from the mill on the off chance. Any hope of a cup of tea?'

Laura smiled to herself and went into the house without so much as a look in Dominic's direction.

I used to wear my hair in long plaits, right down to my waist. Each morning before I went downstairs for breakfast, Mother or one of the girls would brush with long, regular strokes and then help me plait, fingers over fingers, pulling tight on each strand, nothing stray, nothing uncared for, and then tie big silk bows on the ends; green bows on school days that matched the gym slip ı had to wear; more cheerful ones at weekends.

For parties I was allowed to keep my hair loose, held back from my face by a velvet band, hanging straight and shining down my back; velvet dress, lace collar, tight white socks and patent leather shoes shining like my hair. That, of course, was before I had a mind of my own.

Sometimes he would collect me from parties; this would put the cat among the pigeons, all right.

'Senator!' I would hear their voices. 'It's the Senator. Won't you step inside and have a little . . . ha ha . . . just a little . . . it's a cold evening out . . . drop. Laura can wait a minute. Run back on in to the party, dear, your daddy's just going to. . . .' He would give me a little smile and disappear into some sanctum where only men were welcome . . . or so it seemed to me. My mother was never treated with such deference. I always got the feeling they didn't want her over the threshold, staring perhaps, evaluating, making judgments in her head.

I was sitting beside him in the car one winter evening; his face was still smiling the senatorial smile, his breath smelt of the whiskey they had pressed on him. The triumph of the successful wrapped him – as my velvet party cloak that had belonged to Mother when she was my age, wrapped me. We were both warm.

He took my hand and held it in his warm hand for a moment, and then put it on his leg. Quite high up on his leg; I remember, because in school we had been learning about the ball and socket that formed the hip, and I thought of the ball and socket as we drove in silence. Sometimes when he didn't need his left hand for driving, he pressed it on top of my hand, pressed the two hands deep down into his flesh, and he smiled.

I could see the smile there on his lips in the almost dark. I loved him then. I loved his smiling confidence. I loved the warmth of his power.

'Do you think your man's a pouf?'

They were sitting by the open drawing room window drinking their coffee. The sky was bleached by the last rays of the sun; shadows were long and just beginning to fade.

There are so few times of real silence, she had just been thinking to herself, when he spoke.

'Who?'

She was a little startled, not just by the question but by the sound of his voice.

'You know. The schoolmaster chappie, the spoiled priest.'

'Dominic,' she said. 'I wouldn't have thought so. Whatever gave you that idea?'

'I don't know. He's a bit odd, isn't he? The way he sort of lurks around. You wouldn't know what was in his head.'

'His father's dying. I know that's going on in his head.'

'Ah,' said Maurice.

'Such peace,' she said.

'"Dropping from the veils of the morning to where the cricket sings, There midnight's all aglimmer and noon a purple glow, And evening full of the linnet's wings."'

She laughed gently.

'Imagine that.'

'It's the only poem I ever learned at school. The only poem I remember having learned at school. It's good to be able to trot it out occasionally. Thank you for the opportunity.'

'You speak the lines trippingly.'

'Do you think he has the hots for you?'

'Who? Oh . . . good heavens, no. His father's dying. He's lonely. He doesn't know what to do with his life. I'm just an ear, a maker of tea.'

A dog barked in the distance and she shivered.

'Cold?' he asked. 'Like me to get you a coat?'

She shook her head. 'A goose walking over my grave.'

'I love moments like this. Do you, Laura?'

'Yes.'

'Dote.'

He put out his hand and took hers. He plaited his fingers through hers and they sat there in silence again, looking at the last of the day.

'Dote, petal, blossom, dearie!'

She was standing on the grass outside the back door eating yogurt from a plastic carton and planning her day. A haze drifting from the sea lay on the hill; it was going to be hot. She was in her dressing gown and her hair hung tangled and unbrushed down to her waist.

She didn't answer his call.

He switched the radio from the Third Programme, Haydn, to the Radio Eireann early morning news headlines.

'. . . the Secretary of State for. . . .'

'Laura.'

'. . . Northern Ireland will be. . . .'

'You'll catch cold.'

He was at the door behind her.

'. . . holding talks today with. . . .'

'Bare feet.'

'Nobody ever got a cold. . . .'

'. . . the Minister for Foreign Affairs. . . .'

'The grass is wet.'

'Dew. Nobody ever got a cold from dew.'

'. . . in London this afternoon.'

'Breakfast.'

'In the oven.'

'. . . it is expected. . . .'

She laughed.

'What, dote? What's so funny?'

'It is expected. . . . They're always saying things like that. They all think they're so clever. They all think they're in the know.'

'Breakfast!'

'I'll be in in a minute.'

'The Minister for Agriculture and his special adviser, Mr Maurice Quinlan, will be flying to. . . .'

'That's you.'

She turned round and looked at him.

True enough, he was in his best suit.

'. . . Brussels today for talks with. . . .'

'That's me.'

He went back into the kitchen.

She followed him in.

'Brussels?'

'I only knew last night, dote. The Minister. . . .'

She switched off the radio.

He sat down at the table and waited for her to put his breakfast in front of him.

'It's just an overnighter. I'll be back tomorrow. All things being equal, I'll be back tomorrow. I knew you wouldn't mind. The Minister. . . . Laura, where is my breakfast?'

She bent down and opened the bottom oven of the Aga and took out his breakfast.

I hate fried eggs, she thought, as she brought it round the table and put it in front of him.

'None for you?'

He always said that.

She ignored it and poured herself a cup of tea.

'Of course I don't mind. I just like to be told . . . and what's all this about being a special adviser . . . ? You never told me anything about that. What do you advise specially on?'

'That's just Radio Eireann getting things wrong as usual. It's all to do with cereal subsidies . . . boring things like that. You wouldn't. . . .'

'Probably not.'

'He just calls me in from time to time to bounce ideas off me.'

'Bounce,' she said quietly.

'I have my connections into Europe, you know. . . .'

'Bounce.'

'I can keep him genned up better, in some ways, than the civil servants. I have a. . . .'

'Bounce.'

She held her cup with both hands up in front of her face. She saw him, spruce and every inch a special adviser, through the steam that drifted up.

'. . . though I say it myself, a broader view.'

'Bounce.'

'What?'

'Great. That's great. I hope you have a very interesting time.'

'The discussion should be lively. . . . Of course, I don't speak officially, that is . . . just keep the Minister on the right track. You know the sort of thing.'

'You'll end up a senator. Like my father.'

He laughed.

He drew his knife through the centre of the egg and yellow yolk spread out over the plate.

'I hardly think so. Your father was a different kettle of fish. Your father was a patriot as well as a. . . .'

He put a forkful of egg and fried bread into his mouth and chewed. Yellow glistened on his lower lip.

'. . . man of political vision and a. . . .'

'Oh, shut up,' she said. 'I'm sorry I ever mentioned him.'

'. . . great man. Where do you think I would be now if it hadn't been. . . .'

'Where, oh where?'

'. . . for your father?'

'Egg on your chin. Dribbling egg. You'd have managed.'

He dabbed at his chin with his napkin.

'You didn't need my father. You'd have got on in the world without him.'

'Oh, I don't know.'

He looked at the yellow stain on the napkin, and gave another little rub to his chin.

'You have what it takes. That's what he used to say about you.'

'Did he really?'

He looked pleased.

'I thought he just liked my father . . . you know, thought I was O.K. because of my father. . . .'

'You have what it takes. He wanted a son. Do all men want sons?'

Carefully he drew the knife across the egg again.

'Just take care,' he said, and lifted the fork to his mouth. He chewed in silence.

She drank her tea in silence.

Silence was like the splint that held a broken limb tight, she thought – prevented pain, prevented truth, prevented dislocation, falling apart. Long live silence!

I didn't hear him coming.

Only his shadow falling across the page of my book made me look up. He stood tall, like a giant between me and the sun.

I sat on the bottom step of the summerhouse and squinted up at him. I couldn't see his face, just this black giant keeping the light from me.

'Where's your mother?'

I shrugged. I was still angry with them both. I felt no reason to pretend that I was now happy with their decision.

'Out in that damn boat, I suppose. Hey?'

'I haven't seen her since breakfast.'

'Damn boat.'

He moved slightly, and the sun flooded over me again. My eyes were dazzled for a moment and in that moment he sat down beside me and took my hand in his.

The book dropped from my knee onto the grass.

'Always reading, your nose always stuck in a book,' he said in a casual voice. 'You're upset.'

I said nothing.

He let go of my hand and pulled a large white handkerchief from his breast pocket and blotted at his forehead.

It was a perfect summer day. Grasshoppers tick-ticked in the haze-held silence.

He was always affected by the heat. The only times I ever saw him lose a little of his poise was in the heat: sweat would shine and bubble on his forehead and slide down the sides of his nose. His formal clothes would look uneasy on him. His hands became moist to touch.

'I . . . we . . . only want to do what is the best for you. We . . . of course, we.'

I said nothing.

I watched him blot the moisture from his skin, forehead, nose, the back of his neck; then, before he tucked the handkerchief back into his pocket, he carefully wiped the palms of his hands.

'Of course, we.' He repeated the words.

'Mummy said I could go if you said yes. Mummy said. . . .'

'We have discussed it. We have agreed upon it. If your mother ever said yes, she says it no longer. She recognises now how ill-considered that word was. The convent is as good a school as you'll find in this country. You know that I only want the best for you. I will speak to Reverend Mother about that little problem you told your mother about. You will have no more bother like that. I . . . we . . . want you to stay here, with us, in this place, your home. It is best that you should stay in your home.'

I bent down and picked up my book.

I opened it and attempted to read the words, any words, but they dazzled and leapt in front of my eyes.

'Her, and her bloody boat,' he said, after a long silence.

The words dazzled. The grasshoppers. . . .

Small clumps of uncut grass rustled.

Everything around me in that summer moment stirred.

I stared at the page.

He spoke.

I didn't hear his words, just the persuasive drone of his voice, and the grasshoppers.

Tick-tick-tick.

Like time rustling past.

I felt him move beside me, felt the heat of his grey-suited body. He put his arm round my shoulders and pulled me towards him till my head rested against his chest. My fingers clutched for safety at the buoyant cover of the book. My head was bent away from him, staring still towards the pages. His hand rummaged in my hair. His warm lips pressed down towards the nape of my neck.

'Oh, Laura.' He whispered the words. I felt the

heat of the words on my neck. 'Have pity on me.'

His hand crept like some cautious, preying animal across my shoulder.

In the distance a dog barked.

Pekoe. Pekoe barked.

'Mummy's back,' I said.

'Of course.'

He let go of me.

I leant for a moment longer against his chest, listening to the beating of his heart thudding in my ears.

'Yes. Mummy must be back.'

He pushed me away as he spoke and then stood up.

He pulled the handkerchief from his pocket and patted again and again at his face.

Forehead, cheeks, mouth, neck, forehead, hands, neck. He stood, a giant between myself and the sun.

'Your mother. . . .' He blotted out the next words with the handkerchief.

'If you're looking for Mummy, hadn't you better go and find her?'

He nodded.

The dog barked in the distance.

'That's all sorted out, then?'

He put his handkerchief away again.

'About school and that. Sorted out? I'll tell her it's all sorted out. We'll have no more talk about you leaving home.'

He turned and walked away across the grass.

The telephone rang.

She reached out and lifted the receiver.

'Yes?'

It was still dark, the rectangles of the windows barely paler than the room itself.

'Laura?'

It wasn't Maurice.

'Who?'

'It's Dominic.'

'Oh. . . . Do you know. . . .?'

'He's dead.'

'Who?'

'Dad. He. . . .'

'Oh.'

'. . . died. They. . . .'

'I'm sorry.'

'. . . just rang to say. . . .'

'Very sorry.'

'About half an hour ago. Peacefully. Just. . . .'

'Where are you?'

'. . . in his sleep . . . never knew. . . .'

'That's the best way.'

'. . . a thing. . . .'

'Where? Dominic. Answer me. Where are you?'

'Here . . . at the school. The matron's just giving me a cup of tea. The phone. . . .'

'That's good of. . . .'

'. . . woke her. She woke me. I was asleep.'

'So was I.'

'Laura.'

'Yes?'

'Can I come round?'

'What?'

'Can I come round?'

'Now?'

'I don't want you to make tea or anything. I don't need anything like that. I just want. . . .'

He put down the receiver.

She made tea anyway.

She needed it herself.

Telephones should be switched off at night.

All news, whether bad or good, should wait till morning.

With the dawn chorus, telephones could start to ring again; we could then be surprised by the night's events; births, deaths, wars, revolutions.

Having made the tea, she didn't want it.

She poured a mug and left it steaming on the kitchen table. She stood wrapped in a blanket like a Navajo, waiting to hear the sounds of his steps, the turning of the handle, feel the breath of night air move with him through the door.

She hoped he wouldn't cry.

Equilibrium, balance, calm.

She put another mug on the table and then remembered his words and put it back in the press again.

Equilibrium, balance, calm.

There was a tap of knuckles on the door.

'In,' she called without moving.

His face was white.

He looked as if he had already cried. His eyes were sunk deep into his head.

'I just want to sleep,' he said. 'I don't want tea, sympathy, conversation, anything like that. Could you just let me have a bed?'

She nodded.

He followed her out of the kitchen and along the passage.

The flags were cold under her bare feet; his feet shuffled like an old man's feet behind her. Her body gave a little shudder and she pulled the rug tighter round her.

Pale light from the windows patterned the hall

floor and the stairs. It must be getting on for five, she thought, judging by the light.

She crossed the landing to the room that had been hers all those years ago and opened the door.

'Here,' she said. 'No one will disturb you here. Sleep well.'

He moved past her into the room without a word.

She closed the door and went back to bed.

I locked the door.

Every night I locked the door and every night I would hear his soft footsteps across the landing, hear the sound of the handle turning, hear his breathing.

Or maybe it was my imagination.

Maybe I heard none of those things.

Maybe he came home after a dinner or a meeting, just as he had always done when Mother was alive, had a nightcap in his study, and did half an hour's work before going to bed. Maybe then he climbed the stairs, sometimes mumbling to himself, sometimes singing a bar or two of some Victorian ballad. Maybe he went to his room and closed the door and never came out again, never crossed the landing in his bare feet, turned the handle gently, leaned his shoulder against the door, hoping against hope that this time it would give.

Maybe he never had whispered, Have pity on me.

Maybe he never cried my name as he scratched on the door with a fingernail.

Maybe, as my mother said to me, I am crazy.

It was well into the afternoon when he came down to the summerhouse to find her.

She was scraping moss off the steps with an old kitchen knife.

The summerhouse, now that it was all uncovered, no longer looked mysterious, but merely like a neglected, dispirited ruin: there was a smell of decay and rotted wood; there was fungus growing in the angles of the balcony that ran around the wooden structure; the windows were grey with cobwebs and dust, dead flies and spiders; the door looked swollen and impossible to open.

Above all this the Falconeri was in full bloom; rich substantial flowers, leaves long and lustrous.

'You've done it.'

She stood up. 'There's a lot of clearing still to do at the back. I think there are probably some quite nice shrubs there, if it's not too late to save them. How are you? Did you sleep at all?'

He looked more composed than he had in the early hours of the morning.

'Like a log. I'm sorry I did that on you. Really sorry. I couldn't think of anything else to do. . . . I had no other place to go.'

'Forget it. What are friends for?'

He stared past her at the house. 'You've done great work.'

'Head down, bum in the air. Nothing to it,' she said. 'Have you had breakfast?'

'Oh, shut up, Laura . . . don't be motherly. . . . Apart from anything else it's half past three.'

She waved the knife in the air.

'Let's open the door', he said. 'I think this is the moment. Don't you?'

'It's going to be horrid. I'm really quite scared about opening it.'

'If you'd stop brandishing that knife round, we could try.'

She put the knife into her pocket and they went up the three steps and crossed the balcony. He turned the door handle and gave a little push.

'It's locked.'

'No. It definitely couldn't be locked. I don't remember there ever being a key, for heaven's sake. It's just stuck. Brute force will be needed.'

She put her shoulder against the door and heaved.

He put his shoulder against the door and heaved.

'It's locked,' he repeated.

'Don't be silly. There isn't even a blinking keyhole.'

'Then the catch must be jammed. Here, give me the knife.'

She took the knife from her pocket and handed it to him. He bent down and scraped somewhat ineffectually at the space between the frame and the door.

'If you put the knife into the crack just below the handle and give it a. . . .'

'That's what I'm doing,' he said rather crossly.

The knife jammed. He couldn't get it to move either up or down, in or out.

She sat down on the steps. 'Leave it for a while. These things always sort themselves out if you leave them alone for a while.'

He continued to pull at the knife.

'Tell me. . . .' she said.

He gave a rattle at the handle and the knife fell to the ground with a clatter and the door opened a crack. Sticking on the swollen floor boards, it scraped and groaned as he pushed it inch by inch open.

'You're right about the smell, it's foul.'

He stepped through the doorway into the darkness.

She stood on the balcony for a moment, unwilling to follow him in.

'I was astonished and flattered,' she heard her mother's voice and the drone of a bee in the afternoon silence, 'when your father picked on me. He was of course the new nobility. Yes, new nobility. Energetic. Powerful. Some people even say heroic. Such a litany of words I could use for him. He chose me.' She laughed. 'And how could I say no? Answer me that.'

'Don't you want to come in?'

Dominic stuck his head out of the door and called to her.

'Laura?'

'Yes.'

She took a step towards the door.

Her mother's laughter was still in the air.

'Answer me that.'

Nervously she pushed her way through the door. The air was mouldy, the floorboards slightly spongy under her feet.

'Ugh.'

'I think we should try and open some windows . . . let in some light. See over there. . . . I think you're right about the mouldering deck chairs.'

There was a crash. 'I think I've just encountered some of them.'

'Do take care.'

'Have a care, Lord Kildare, Fiacch will do, what Fiacch will dare. . . .'

She stood just inside the door waiting for her eyes to adjust. The five windows were grey patches in the darkness. Something stirred over by the far wall. Dominic was fiddling with the nearest window.

'I think there may be something. . . .'

'Bloody cobwebs,' he muttered. 'Follow me up to Carlow.'

'Do you think it's a rat?'

'Have a care. . . .'

'Or what? Dominic?'

He pulled the window open and air burst into the little house and a bar of sunshine lit the stack of deck chairs and some dusty leaves on the floor. He moved on towards the next window.

'. . . Lord Kildare. . . .'

'Or what?'

'Probably a rat. The floor is full of holes and there's a ratlike smell.'

As he struggled with the next window there was a sudden cracking of glass and shards tinkled onto the floor.

'Damn.'

'I don't like rats.'

'Then retreat. Make a strategic withdrawal. I will deal with whatever manifests itself.'

Every time he moved, dust was disturbed, and rose and shimmered and glittered in the light that now poured in through three windows.

She remained standing unhappily by the door.

Memories stirred with the dust; laughter, the drift of voices.

Why have I resurrected this, she wondered.

No one must know.

Whispered words.

Ever know.

Have pity on me.

Your mother must never know.

Your mother will punish you.

Your mother will never forgive. . . .

Never forgive.

Forgive.

A hand brushed her bare shoulders, gripped tight her streaming hair. . . .

'I can't get at that last one to open it without shifting all that stuff in the corner. There seems to be a sofa or something under those deck chairs . . . and probably the rat too. This will do for the time being.'

'Yes. Thank you.'

'It's great. It'll be great. It just needs scrubbing and a bit of paint.'

'Yes.'

'We can take all this junk out and have another bonfire. A last bonfire.'

She smiled. 'Yes.'

She turned and went out into the sun. He followed her out and down the steps and then bent down and cleaned his hands on the grass.

'You may have to put a new floor in. We'll be able to see better when the place is cleared.'

'Yes.'

She sat down on the grass and stretched her legs out in front of her.

'You don't sound full of enthusiasm.'

'It's the past . . . you know . . . bogies . . . things that are perhaps best left alone. We paint our own picture of the past. Perhaps. . . .'

'Your mother . . . is her presence troubling you here?'

'When is your father's funeral?'

He sat down beside her. He wiped his hands once more on the grass, feeling the cool dampness sliding through his fingers.

'I'm sorry about last night.'

'That's all right. I hope I wasn't too crabbed.'

'Have a care, Lord Kildare. . . .'

He sang the words softly, his fingers moving backwards and forwards on the grass.

'I was rather wretched. You see . . . they seem to think it's my fault.'

'They? Who are they to think such a thing?'

She put out her hand and caught his creeping fingers and held them tight.

'My sisters.'

'Such rubbish.'

'Lena . . . that's my sister. . . .'

Laura nodded.

'. . . she rang to tell me. . . . Lena.'

She moved herself over beside him and put an arm round his shoulders.

'People don't always know what they're saying at moments of distress.'

'She made herself quite plain. "This wouldn't have happened," she said, "if you hadn't come and upset him like you did. Detta agrees with me." Then she handed the phone to Detta. Detta said, I mean she was crying . . . yes . . . she was crying but she said, "I agree with every word Lena has just said." That's all quite clear, isn't it? That's what they believe.'

'Your father was ancient. Your father was very, very ill . . . your father was. . . . What I'm trying to say is that your father's death had nothing to do with you, and your sisters are wicked to suggest that it had.'

He shook his head. 'Maybe she's right. Maybe he'd still be lying there alive, if I hadn't gone to see him. I will never know.'

'It doesn't matter.'

'"Don't bother coming to the funeral," she said.'

'I will leave this country.'

His hands were clenched into fists, his arms and shoulders rigid. His skin beneath her hand was burning hot.

'I don't suppose it's much different anywhere else.'
'"Don't bother coming to the funeral."'
'You'll feel better tomorrow. Able to. . . .'
'I thought we all loved each other.'
'You do, I'm sure you do.'
'Have a care, Lord Kildare. . . .'
She took up the song.
'Fiacch will do what Fiacch will dare. . . .'
He crumpled into her lap, asleep, crying, dead perhaps? She didn't know. She sang on, and stroked his hair, and the summer and time ticked by.

I never went in the boat with her.

The sea has always frightened me.

I like to feel my feet firm on the ground.

I hate the dislocation of horizon and sky and water, all, it seems to me, moving in different directions at the same time.

I swim; of course I swim, sedately mind you, parallel to the shore, never out of my depth. I worry about cramps and undertows, sudden squally gusts of wind that might sweep me away from the safety of the land.

Maurice laughs at me.

He dives, his body arcs, arches perfectly, cuts the water like a sabre. He swims straight out to sea until all I can see sometimes is his head, and sometimes the flash of an arm when the sun catches it as it rises and falls.

He is greatly admired.

I admire him for that; for allowing himself to be admired, for smiling, laughing, clamping his hand onto people's shoulders, making them feel they are his friends.

'He has style, the lad.' My mother said that evening after they had been to tea. 'More than can be said for his parents.'

'Mmmm. Quinlan's sound,' said my father from behind his newspaper.

'How? Sound? What does sound mean?'

'Politically and financially. Very sound. None better.'

'He looks like a crook.'

'My dear woman, you've no idea what you're talking about. You expect people to have thin faces and ride horses . . . speak with marbles in their mouths . . . let me tell you something about that lot . . . they're crooks too, only they're unsuccessful. They've lost. Your swanky lot. Lost. And about time too.'

He rattled at the paper for a few moments.

'That lad of his, whatever his name is . . . he's doing well enough at college. I think I'll try to get him to come into the mill. He has his head screwed on. He's at Trinity.' He laughed. 'God, but times have changed. Yes, you're right. He has a bit of style. I think Joe Quinlan would be happy with the lad being offered something like that.'

I loved him.

Father.

Yes.

He was my warm and lovely god.

My safe haven.

My High King.

My tower of strength.

For bonny sweet Robin is all my joy.

She laughed too much.

I don't mean wild, rambunctious laughter, healthy laughter, but mocking laughter. I could see her mocking him with her eyes, with her little

throwaway sentences; I could feel the arrows stinging me as they stung him.

I loved her, but I never felt safe with her as I did
with him.

I was aware of my aloneness when I was with
her, but never with him. I was a part of his glowing
life.

I never went in the boat with her.

I preferred to keep the ground under my feet.

'I presumed you must be down here. What on
earth are you doing?'

Maurice walked across the grass towards them.

'You're back?'

'Of course I'm back. What's the matter with him?'

The shadows of the trees were longer now, the
sun slipping towards the west.

'His father died last night. He's a bit . . . well, he
just fell asleep and I hadn't the heart to wake him
up. How was Brussels?'

'Grimmish. I see you've finished your exca-
vations.' He walked towards the steps.

'It's recovered . . . perhaps I should say uncovered, but there's still a long way to go.'

He went up the steps cautiously and put his head
through the door.

'Ugh.'

'You'll have to use your imagination now. One
day it will be superb.'

'I'll get a couple of men from the mill to come
down and clear it out for you, if you like. Burn all
that rubbish.'

'Yes, thank you. I'd like that.'

'It'll be lovely, dote, when it's all painted up,
refurbished. Lovely.'

'And if Shamie Doyle could do something to the floor. Fill up the rat holes, fix the rotten boards.'

'Absolutely.'

'I've still got to clear back as far as the stream, then I'll have to decide what to plant. I think an abundance of azaleas and perhaps acers along the water, and some more willows. What do you think?'

'That's your province, dote. I don't know a chestnut from a water spaniel.'

'In five years' time you won't recognise it.'

His shoes were city shining, with a pattern of tiny holes punched on the uppers, his socks maroon silk.

He came and stood beside her, looking down at the man lying in her lap.

'He looks dead.'

'He's breathing. He's just dead tired.'

'He's a dismal creature.'

'Ssssh.'

'I get so bored with the dismal people of the world.'

'Ssh, Maurice.'

'I'd better take a run over to the office just to check that everything's O.K. I won't be long. Don't let's eat too late. I'm tired.'

He put his hand out and touched her hair.

'Dote.'

He walked away across the grass and through the trees; one of his shoes squeaked slightly as he went.

I wish I loved you, she thought as she watched him go.

No, perhaps I'm better off as I am. If I loved you perhaps I wouldn't be able to bear the smooth lies, the false smiles, the dissembling.

Dominic moved, he shifted his head sideways and then heaved his body around so that he lay, his head still on her knees, staring up into her face.

'The sun has gone.'

'Yes.'

'I have imprisoned you here for ever so long. I'm sorry.'

'That's all right.'

He reached up a hand and began to pull the pins and clips from her hair.

She didn't say a word, nor did she make any move to stop him. She just sat like a statue, staring at the wedding tree across the grass from them, hearing the pins drop to the ground, feeling the weight of her hair as it began to unfold and slip down across her shoulders and finally tumble like a dark silk curtain around them both.

He lay still, then.

'Have you ever cut it?' he asked. 'I mean really cut it, not just a sort of tidying operation.'

'Yes, once. Right off, like a boy.'

'Why did you do such a silly thing?'

'I was punishing someone. I was seventeen. I couldn't think of any other way to do it.'

'Seventeen.' He laughed. 'When I was seventeen I was in the seminary.'

'Then I went to France. Did you know that? I spent nearly two years in France. I didn't think anyone knew where I was for two years.'

'In the seminary. Angry and ashamed of myself.'

'I worked for a family in Orleans. Minded the children . . . you know, that sort of thing. I'd never done anything like that in my life.'

'. . . because I didn't want to be there and I hadn't the bloody guts to say so.'

'They were really nice. Decent. I fell on my feet

with them. Some people have rotten luck with that sort of thing.'

'I used to think they'd suss me out. Send me home with a flea in my ear and a letter to my father, but they never did.'

'They had three nice kids and a baby . . .'

'I was a good actor. Took them all for a ride.'

'Marie José, that was the baby's name. She was sweet. . . . I used to say to myself, What I'm learning here will come in handy when I have my own.'

'Passed all my exams with flying colours.'

'I used to sing her songs to get her off to sleep. Hushabye Baby . . . that sort of thing. I was quite happy then. I was safe. That was a great feeling.'

'I heard what he said. I wasn't asleep. I heard. . . .'

'Maurice?'

'I suppose I am a bit dismal.'

'Don't bother about that. He just says things like that sometimes. He doesn't really mean them.'

He took hold of a strand of her hair and twisted it round his finger.

'He likes fun, you know. I'm not exactly fun. I think I drive him to despair at times. If you're not working or sleeping, fun's the name of the game for him.'

She began to feel on the ground around her for the hairpins. 'He's all right; I'm not complaining. He's very kind. He suits me fine. I suit him fine. No problem.'

'Why did you marry him?'

She pulled her hair away from him and began to pin it up behind her head.

'You've lost all my pins.'

'It doesn't matter.'

'When I was about fourteen, my father used to joke about it. "A fine young husband for my girl," he used to say. "A handsome pair you'll make one day, walking down the aisle together." Silly things like that. I only laughed. My mother laughed, too. But later on he thought the better of it.'

He rolled himself off her knee and sat up.

'Stiff,' he said, moving his legs gingerly, cracking his shoulders back and forth. 'Age creeping on. Why did he think the better of it?'

She stabbed a couple of pins into her hair.

'Oh, I just think he thought, after I came back from France, that I could look after him for ever. The traditional Irish daughter. The sacrificial lamb. This is my house, you see. When I got married to Maurice he had to leave. Fend for himself. I thought he might marry again. He was a very attractive man, you know. He should have married again. Some county lady fallen on hard times would have suited him nicely. He could have railed at her for being a Prod and at the same time he'd have enjoyed the benefits.'

'Benefits?'

'Yes. You know . . . that mythological edge they have over everyone else. The glamour of being an endangered species. But what he liked was the air of history, of knowing where you came from . . . crests on the spoons, book plates, family portraits, all those museumlike objects collected down the years, centuries, by grandfathers and great-grandfathers. We use those artefacts every day, we live fairly comfortably with the ghosts of the past. It's quite seductive, that. You can't buy that. He became a part of it through me, not through my mother. I was part of that chain and I was also his, so that made him. . . .'

A sudden breeze hurried round the clearing,

stirring the grass and making the leaves rustle and whisper.

She shivered.

He picked up another couple of hairpins and handed them to her.

'Thanks.' She pushed them into her hair.

He got up and held out a hand to her.

'I'll go up to town tonight. I'll stay there until after the funeral. If they won't have me at home, I'll stay with friends.'

'Is that what you were working out when you were lying there?'

'I suppose so, but I only just knew it this moment, just as I said it.'

'You can borrow my car.'

'That's kind.'

'It just sits there. I never use it.'

'Would you come with me?'

She was startled by the request.

'No . . . I hate funerals. I don't know your family. No. I would find it fearsome.'

'I'm going to find it pretty fearsome, too.'

She took his hand and they walked towards the house.

'My bum is soaking,' she said. 'I'll probably get rheumatism, a chill in my kidneys, piles. . . .'

He laughed.

Once they left the shadowing tree, the sun was on their backs as they climbed up the field towards the house. The cattle had gathered in one corner and stood there whisking their tails to discourage midges; they looked as if they were waiting for something to happen.

Maurice came out of the kitchen door as they arrived. He held a glass in his hand. He held it up in their direction; ice and lemon bobbed and clinked.

'Drink?'

'No, thanks,' said Dominic.

'Whiskey? Glass of wine? Glass of wine, dote?'

'I must be off,' said Dominic.

'I'm lending him my car. He has to go to Dublin.'

'Sorry to hear about your father. Sad times and all that. Had he been ill?'

'Yes. Yes. . . . He's been dying for. . . .'

'Not unexpected, then. A shock, though. Always a shock. Sorry. The tank is full. I checked before I went away. I always check before I go away, just in case of emergencies. Laura's so. . . .'

'I'll get the keys.'

'. . . scatty sometimes.'

Laura went in through the kitchen door and the two men stood side by side. Maurice jiggled the glass in his hand for a moment and then took a long drink.

'I'm sorry,' he repeated.

'Thank you,' said Dominic.

'When's the . . . ah . . . funeral?'

'Tomorrow. Sacred Heart, Donnybrook.'

'Know it well.'

Laura came out of the house with the keys in her hand. She held them out towards Dominic.'

'The car's in the garage. I'll show you. I'm in no hurry for it back. You can keep it a few days if you wish.'

He took the keys and ducked his head towards Maurice. 'Well. . . .'

'Toodloo. I hope everything goes all right. Not too much. . . .' He looked down at his glass and cleared his throat. 'Sorry again,' he said eventually.

One of the beasts was found dead in the field this morning.

Maybe that is what they were waiting for, I said to myself when I heard the news: death.

Yes, I suppose so. For a while, as they whisked their tails to discourage the midges, they felt death's approach.

From the window where I am sitting, I can see the local vet and Shamie and two strangers, men from the Department, I think, crouched round the dwindled corpse.

Father had done his dwindling before he died; death for him was a smoothing out of the anxiety scarring his face. Fear would be a better word. Even after he had received the Last Rites, that fear was still tormenting him.

Forgive me.

Yes.

Forgive me.

Forgive.

Echoes.

I have often wondered since if the hatred I felt for him showed in my eyes, my voice.

Forgive me.

Yes.

> Of her bones are coral made.
> Those are pearls that were her eyes.
> Nothing of her that doth fade
> But doth suffer a sea change.

Yes.

Pearls.

That is how I see her in my mind.

> Sea nymphs hourly ring her knell.
> Ding dong bell, pussy's in the well.

I can feel the walls gathering round me.
Impenetrable.

I have been, well, grasping life now for weeks,
perhaps even months. I don't remember.

I remember that book I was reading, full of life
and explosions of joy, full of richness. I felt for a
time filled also with that richness.

Such feelings drain away.

Tomorrow I know I will want to die.

It's as if there were a stopper somewhere in my
body, and when it is pulled out I become slowly
drained of hope, love, confidence, even the ability
to feel pain; I become an empty skin; I do not even
have the energy to kill myself. I long for the safe,
lapping waters of the womb, darkness.

Tomorrow. It will be like that tomorrow.

Maurice came into the room and looked at her
sitting in the chair by the window. He walked across
the room and stood beside her, looking down at
the four men and the body of the heifer.

'They're from the Department,' he said. 'It's bet-
ter to be sure than sorry. She may have eaten yew.
I don't know. I don't like these sudden deaths.
You're not dressed?'

She shook her head.

He put a hand out and touched her shoulder.

'You're pale. Are you all right, dote?'

'I'm all right.' Her voice was dull. Just above her
right eye a little pulse throbbed.

'I'll run your bath for you. You'll feel better then.
It's been hot. Too hot for you. You sat in the sun

all yesterday afternoon. That was foolishness. That's not good for you, you know.'

He moved away, talking as he went, into the bathroom. She could hear him turning on the tap, the water flowing into his voice.

Prattle, she said to herself. Kind prattle.

'They'll be moving her in a minute. Shamie's gone to get the tractor. There will have to be a postmortem. I'll make coffee. When you come down, it will be ready for you. A nice hot cup of coffee. You will come down, won't you? Laura. You will come down?'

'Yes,' she said. 'I will come down.'

He looked at her with anxiety for a moment and then left the room.

She listened to his footsteps in the passage; the sound left a track in her brain.

She stood up and putting out her hand she grasped the tassled end of the cord and slowly pulled the cream-coloured blind down, then moved across the room and did the same thing with the other window.

'The light hurts my eyes.'

She said the words aloud.

Hurts

my

eyes.

Echoes.

Echoes hurt my eyes.

One of the men in the field laughed, and the sound drifted through the blinds. She went into the bathroom and closed the door.

An hour later Maurice found her sitting on the chair by the bath, the silver snail tracks of tears lying on her face. The bath water was cold.

Gently he washed her face, and then led her to her bed.

'Dote,' he said. 'Rest a while. Everything will be all right. A little sleep and then. . . .'

He pushed her down onto the bed and pulled the covers over her.

She lay there staring up and seeing nothing except darkness.

'It always takes so long,' she said.

Days pass.

Nights.

Each has its own darkness.

He comes and goes; sometimes the echo of his steps hurts me; sometimes I don't hear a thing, I just see his figure moving in the twilight.

I eat because they bring me food.

I never feel hunger, but I feel the need to eat the food they bring me – just to pacify them in some way, acknowledge their gracefulness in caring for me.

They talk to me or to each other, believing, I have no doubt, in the therapy of good humour. Teresa or Bridie or Katie or Nellie.

I don't listen.

I try to eat what they bring me.

Their words are like handfuls of pebbles thrown in a stream, splattering, sprawling for a moment on the surface of the water, and then disappearing for ever.

I get up several times a day and go to the bathroom. It is like going on a voyage round the world; sometimes I fill the bath with water and then haven't the energy left to step into it. I sit and look at the still water. I sit with my hands folded in my lap and look at the still water. I will sit there until someone comes and brings me back to my bed.

My head is so full of pain. I would like to scream, but he puts his hand over my mouth. I try to bite his hand, but he presses hard down on my body and the pain cracks in me and the dog barks in the distance or whines outside my door scratching with his claws on the white paint: the lonely dog wanting in, the lonely man, the pain, and my teeth scrabbling to bite his hand.

Such terrible dreams leave me sweating all over. Dreams or memories?

I don't know.

They change the sheets; they cool me with cloths soaked in cold water and then wrung out so they won't drip on the floor and bed.

Sometimes I know it will all end. I will be well again: other times I can't remember such comfortable thoughts at all.

Then Maurice came into the room one day and walked across to the window.

'Rain,' he said. 'Just in time for the harvest. The farmers are going mad all over Ireland.'

He lifted the blind halfway to let her see the rain streaking down from the grey sky.

I must be on the mend, she thought. I am no longer oppressed by the light.

He stood black against the window and rubbed his finger on the glass.

'Don't, Maurice.'

He left the blind the way it was and then walked over to the other window and pulled that blind also halfway up. She could hear clearly now the scattering sound of the rain.

'Six weeks of sunshine. You don't know what you missed. Like the bloody Med.'

He came to the end of the bed and looked down at her.

'I thought we'd have an early harvest. Get all the problems over with early. Relax. Bumper harvest. What a hope. Nature's a bitch.'

He stared at her face for a long time in silence.

'You look more yourself.'

'What does that mean?'

'Alive, I suppose. You have come back to life.'

'I feel ghastly.'

'Yes. You look ghastly, but alive. That's a step. Isn't it, dote?'

He came round to the side of the bed and took her hand in his. He pressed her fingers gently with his thumb.

'You'll be fine now. We'll all be fine. The weather forecast is dreadful.' He put his hand into his pocket. 'Oh, for a spot of the warm South, or something like that. Everything's O.K., dote. No need for you to worry about anything. Rest your mind. That's what Dr McCann says you need to do. Rest your mind. The priesteen is below, by the way. He's been coming every day to sit here with you. Will I send him up or would you rather not?'

She didn't answer.

'I'll send him up. He has a book. He always brings a book. I'll get him to bring up a cup of tea. I'm sure you'd like a cup of tea.'

She didn't answer.

He went to the door.

'First step, dote. That's great, isn't it?'

He opened it and left the room.

I was right to marry him, she thought, even though it was for all the wrong reasons.

'You want to put me out of this house. Sweep me out. My home.'

'Yes,' was all she said.

She stood in his study in front of his desk.

She looked not at his face, but at his hands, lying, fingers spread, in front of the ordered objects on the desk: papers, notebooks, ledgers, a silver inkwell, a porcelain tray filled with sharpened pencils and his fountain pen, a penknife that her mother had given him, a ruler, two India rubbers and some paperclips; there was also a small carriage clock and, near to the spreading hands, a half-full glass of whiskey.

'I will forbid it.'

He stood up and came round the desk towards her. She stepped back, out of reach of his hands.

'Forbid?'

'Yes. I shall not allow. . . .'

'How can you forbid? Father. I am grown up. Anyway, all this was in your head years ago. I remember when he first came down here with his father and mother. I remember it was in your head, then . . . this . . . outcome. I remember Mother. . . .'

'Don't mention your mother.'

'I was still at school. It was before. . . .'

'Don't mention your mother.'

'He drove his father's car down. I remember that. He was so pleased with himself. For heaven's sake, Father, he's practically running the mill. You put him there. You encouraged him. You gave him power so that you could give yourself more time for bloody politics. You taught him how to wheel and deal. So don't tell me now it isn't suitable.'

'You're too young to marry. You're not yet twenty. Too young and that's flat. No. I say no, no, no.'

'I'm going to marry him, Father, so you can save

your breath. You'll have to move out. I mean, out of the house. Quite soon. I don't want you living here with us, even for a week.'

His face had become red with rage.

'Out of my house . . . my home. You are throwing me out of . . . ?'

'It's my house. My home. Remember that.'

He threw his hands in the air. 'What a hard little bitch you have become.'

She didn't say a word, just stared into his eyes. After a moment he looked away. A nerve trembled by the corner of his right eye.

'I have never been alone,' he said at last, his voice low. 'Even those two years you were away in France, I knew you would come back. I lived in the expectation that you would come back to me. That we could. . . .'

'I have no expectations, Father.'

'There are a dozen young men would die to have you.'

'I think not. If they knew. Who wants someone like me? Who wants someone . . . foul, like me?'

He ran past her and out of the room, his well-kept, gentleman's hands clenched over his ears.

'Who would want someone like me?'

Dominic was standing at the end of the bed.

'What?'

He looked apologetic.

'What?' He raised his right hand in salutation. He held a book in his fist.

'I've brought my book. I can just . . . by the window. I see you have the blinds up today. I can just sit quietly. Unless of course you'd rather I went away. I can come back another time. I. . . .'

'It's all right,' she said. 'Don't worry. Sit here on the bed. You can talk to me or read, or read to . . . or even sing me a song if you like.'

He slipped the book into his pocket and sat down cautiously on the bed.

He looked at her right hand, which lay quite still and white on the bedspread. It looked as if no blood moved through it at all; the bones seemed barely covered by the flesh.

He put out his hand and covered hers.

'You're cold. Can I. . . .'

She smiled. 'No. I'm not cold. It's an illusion. Only my hands and my feet are cold; the rest of me is hot, sometimes burning. Talk to me. I don't want to speak. It's too soon to speak.'

'I came here every day. Sat over. . . .' He nodded towards the window. '. . . there. You never noticed?'

She shook her head.

'I didn't think you would mind. I was so afraid that you too might . . . well . . . like my father. . . . Maurice assured me that it would be all right. Just a question of time, he said. That's all. Just a question of. . . .' He pressed her fingers with his and then let go of her hand, afraid that he might damage it in some way.

'All the summer has gone now. Do you realise that? It's getting darker in the evenings. Soon it will be September. We've cleaned up your summer-house for you. It's all ready now. Just needs a coat of paint. We've put in a new floor, windows, all that. We thought – we discussed it, you know, Maurice and I – that we should do that. I've been free. Summer holidays.'

He was silent for a long time. 'We didn't like to paint it in case we chose the wrong colour.' Her eyes were shut and he wondered if she was asleep.

'Maurice said you'd be all right. He told me that you took these turns sometimes. I'd never have guessed. You seemed so. . . . We became quite pally, he and I.'

Rain rattled again on the window.

'Rain. It's a shame you missed all the good weather. So strong, that was what I was going to say. You seemed so strong.'

He touched her hand briefly and then stood up.

'I'm buzzing off now. I don't want to tire you out. I'll be back tomorrow . . . if that's all right.'

She opened her eyes and looked up at him.

'Did your father die?' she asked.

'Yes. Just before you. . . .'

'I'm sorry. I remember now. I'm sorry. Tomorrow. We'll talk about it tomorrow. I'll be up and about tomorrow. I'll surprise you.'

He nodded and left the room.

Bruised. . . . No, unclean.

Marked, marred by uncleanness.

Dirty.

Foul. That was the word I shouted at him.

Defiled.

Stained, smirched.

I carry all those words inside my head.

The colours of bruising move inside me; blue, purple, yellow, black, sometimes red, spreading, hurting when touched.

I shall be well again. I shall be ill again, I shall return and return again to bruising hatred.

The rain beats on the window panes. The trees rustle their summer branches, heavy with leaves and rain.

- 133 -

The sun was shining and a heifer died in the field. I remember that. His father died. My father died.

The sound of the rain hurts my head, batters on the yellow bruising, but I mustn't blame the rain.

No . . . nor the sun for burning me, no.

I must not blame.

'I've run a bath for you, dote.'

Yes.

'I made a list,' she said. 'I must be getting better.'

'You are better. No doubt of that.'

'It wasn't a very nice list, but nonetheless. . . .'

He stood in the bathroom door. He was wearing his going-to-Dublin suit and a blue silk tie. He looked sharp, she thought, that was the word they used nowadays, sharp, unless of course she had been asleep for a hundred years – and then, un-doubtedly, the word sharp would be somewhat out of date.

'Have I been asleep for a hundred years?'

He laughed. 'Good old Laura. What did I tell you? Back to form again. Can you make it to the bathroom?'

She pushed back the bedclothes and suddenly felt free.

'I feel as if I'd been in prison,' she said, slowly swinging her feet over the side of the bed and putting them on the ground.

'If you can manage. . . .'

She stood up.

The room swung a bit, but she remained standing.

'Yes.'

'I'll open the windows. This room stinks of. . . .'

He almost ran across the room. He pulled the blind cord and the blind rattled up to the top of the window and wound itself round the roller. He pushed up the sash. Rain and wind rushed and rattled into the room. He moved on to the second window.

'Shock treatment,' she said, as the wind shook her thin body.

'Therapy,' he said.

'You're going to Dublin?'

'Have to. Have to, dote, I've meetings, appointments, a thousand things to do.'

'You've also been in prison?'

'I suppose you could put it like that. So. . . .'

'I can manage.'

A few spots of rain lay on the shoulders of his pale suit and spattered the floor around his feet.

'I can manage.'

He nodded.

'Yes,' he said. 'I know.'

As the day went on, the wind got up and the heavy trees below the house bowed and shook. There was moaning from time to time in the chimney, and rain drops splattered into the lazy fire.

'Tell me if you want me to go. Tell me if I tire you out.'

She and Dominic sat in her sitting room.

She wore a long black dress and her pale hands moved restlessly, smoothing, plucking, tangling with each other. Her face also was pale and looked thin, and her hair, spread dark down over her shoulders, looked almost too heavy to bear.

'I'll make you a cup of tea this time. Would you like that? A quid pro quo.'

She smiled at him. 'It's all right. The girls are

here. The girls come, you know, when this happens. They hold things together. They are so kind. They know just what to do. They'll bring tea, when they feel it is the right minute.'

'Do you often get ill like this?'

She looked vague. 'From time to time. No. Not often. Don't let's talk about it. You. You talk to me. I find it quite tiring to talk.' She laughed. 'Maurice says that Dr McCann says I should rest my brain. It seems to me my brain rests most of the time. I must have the best-rested brain in Ireland.'

'Maurice never really told me what exactly was the matter.'

'I'm just mad, you know. Didn't you know that? Poor Maurice Quinlan's mad wife. No . . . I do exaggerate a bit. Peculiar. That's the word they use.'

'I've never heard anyone. . . .'

'That's because you're peculiar, too.'

'Am I? I've never thought of myself as anything but very ordinary.'

'What happened?' she asked abruptly.

'Happened? When?'

'After your father died.'

'I don't know that I should. . . .'

'Don't be daft. I'm better. I'm on the road to normality. It wasn't anything to do with you, you know. It just happens . . . the sun maybe . . . ghosts . . . the summerhouse. . . . Yes, it might have been the summerhouse . . . then that poor cow. . . . I never know what triggers off these happenings. It certainly was nothing to do with you.'

'He left me nothing. Not even a silver hairbrush or a photograph.'

'That was pretty crude, really.'

He shrugged.

'I said to my brother afterwards . . . circumnavigating the girls, you see . . . I said . . . my brother Kieron . . . he's the one I told you about. . . .'

'Yes. Yes, I know. The whizz kid in London.'

'It was all strange and like a nightmare. Aunt Margaret looked at me askance . . . and others. . . . Oh yes, some people turned their heads away. I got the cold shoulder, I think that's the right expression, or maybe I was imagining, oversensitive, you know. . . . Well, anyway, after all the drinks and that sort of thing were over, I suggested to Kieron that we should have a word or two.'

Her hands had become still as she listened to him and now lay together, well trained, in her lap.

'I followed him into the old man's study and he sat down at the desk, just like my father used to . . . that got me a bit, I must say. Why so soon, I thought? He looked at me across the desk as my father had, and said, "Well, Dominic, where do you go from here?"'

The gilt clock on the mantelpiece chimed three times, a charming musical sound.

He looked up at the clock and then nervously rubbed his hand across his forehead.

'And you said?' Laura leaned towards him as she asked the question.

'I just told him I would like some pictures of my mother and father and some of us when we were kids at the seaside. Just snapshots, that sort of thing. Nothing else. I mean, just things I could look at and say to myself, It is possible to be happy . . . I was loved . . . these are my people . . . we were happy. Oh fuck it, Laura, I did try. I did what they wanted. It didn't work. I am merely a failure, not a criminal.'

She shook her head.

'What did he say?'

'"You'll have to ask the girls. I wouldn't want to upset the girls. The girls have been so marvellous, so staunch, so loyal. The girls' sensibilities need to be protected." "And what about mine?" I asked, and he smiled at me. He stretched out his hand towards me. He was wearing beautiful amethyst cuff links, just right for a funeral, don't you think? Well, he stretched out his hand to me and said, "Dommie, you know I'd do a lot for you, but we have to protect the girls at this moment. Wait a while, old man. Ask them in a few months' time when they don't feel so raw. Ask them then. That's my advice."'

Dominic took a handkerchief from his pocket and blew his nose.

'That's it, really. That's all that happened,' he said at last. He folded the handkerchief neatly and put it back into his pocket.

'But what did you say? You must have said something.'

'There was this picture of my mother on the desk, and all of us . . . you know, one of those studio pictures. All of us clustered round her, smiling, the girls in their party dresses, Kieron and I brushed and polished. I put my hand out to take it, and he snapped it face down onto the desk. "You heard what I said," was all he said. So I didn't say anything. I just left the room. In fact I left the house. I didn't say goodbye. I went out into the sun. . . . You missed all the sunshine . . . we had weeks of it.'

'Yes.'

'I had your car . . . do you remember that?'

She nodded.

'So I just got into your car and drove away. The sun was shining. I drove with all the windows open. Something got in my eyes. The sun or dust or something got in my . . . I had to stop for a while by the side of the road and wait till I was able to see again. But I got back here all right. That was all. I filled her up with petrol. She's full of. . . .'

'You needn't have bothered. Thank you.'

He walked over to the window and stood looking out at the teeming landscape.

After a long silence he spoke again.

'I have to tell you something . . . a decision I took.'

'Go ahead.'

'I gave in my notice. It's something I've been intending to do for ages. Then, that night, I went straight in to see the Head. I must say he's been very kind. He said I could stay there in my room until term starts.'

'Yes, kind.'

'Food and that, too. It's pretty decent. They have the decorators in up there at the moment. I keep an eye on them from time to time. I do odd jobs.'

'So . . . ?'

He stared in silence out of the window.

'Dominic!'

'Oh, yes.'

He turned round. She couldn't see his face, just the black silhouette of his body against the grey window.

'Term starts next week. I'm leaving then.'

'So soon?'

'Yes.'

'Where are you going? Have you made plans? Have you any notion as to what you're going to do?'

'Would you come with me?'

'I?' She was startled.

'Yes. That's what I would like more than

anything, that you would come away with me. Away from here. We could both start again. I can't say where I will be going until I know that.'

'No. No. No.'

'Why do you say no with such vehemence? I'm all right. I can work hard. I have a good classics degree. Together. . . .'

She held out a hand towards him, but he remained adamantly by the window, so she couldn't see his face.

'I would be useless. I would be such a burden on your back. I would get ill.'

'I could mind you just as well as Maurice does. Anyway, it occurred to me that you might never get ill again if you were to leave this place. Have you ever thought of that?'

'I can't leave this place.'

'That's all in your head. Of course you can, if you want to.'

She shook her head.

He moved at last towards her.

He looked wretched, she thought, just about as wretched as I must look. What a pair we'd make, out in the world.

'Laura, think about it. We might perhaps be happy.'

'I cannot leave this place. After all, what would my mother have to say . . . my grandmother, come to that, if I ran away, abandoned them?'

She laughed.

'Abandoned them.'

'Don't joke.'

'I'm not joking.'

'I know what your mother would have to say. Get out, woman. Be happy, woman. Leave all this behind.'

Laura shook her head. 'She burdened me with it.

She went out and drowned herself when she wasn't able to handle things. I'll tell you something. I won't do that. I'm going to see the whole thing through. Life and all that, so I am, so I am.'

She ran a finger gently over the knuckles of his hand and then suddenly laughed. She threw her head back and laughed. Her frail body shook with the strength of the laughing.

'Did you hear what I've just said? I've never said that aloud before. I doubt if I've even thought it. I always knew there was that way out, I've always recognised that emergency exit. Oh God. I feel so brave to have made a decision.'

'Laura. . . .'

'I hate the name Laura. I can't think why they gave it to me.'

'Laura. . . .'

'Go away now. I'm tired out. I want to sleep. Come back tomorrow and if the sun is shining we'll go and look at the summerhouse. Do you think I will be able walk that far?'

'I'll help you. I'll carry you if need be.'

She shut her eyes in the hope that he would go.

'I thought you were going to die,' he said.

He put out a hand and touched her hair and then she heard him walking across the room and out into the passage.

I always knew that the summer was really over when the little boat was pulled out of the sea by one of the tractors. It looked so ungainly, harnessed onto its trailer, like a swan on land; no grace, no buoyant beauty left.

I remember the smell of seaweed, and the sound of rattling stones as they pulled it up to the shed at the back of the cove. The sails were spread out to dry and then rolled away for the winter months; halyards, sheets, stays were all checked, and either stowed safely in a large wooden box in the shed, or replaced by new ones.

Barnacles and weed were scraped from the hull, oakum was packed into the cracks that opened between the planks when the boat dried out.

Pekoe and I would sit for hours and watch her hammering, scraping, stripping old bubbled paint, both of us happy that she was there with us rather than flying away round the headland, a white bird against the grey speckled sea.

Wind, streaking the sky with colour, shaking the trees and sometimes the house, burrowing in the chimneys; the richness of storms I love, and the flying, heaping leaves; everywhere disturbed colour, nothing still.

That for me is autumn.

When I arrived home from France it was autumn.

He met me at the airport.

I saw him tall among the crowds, unexpected.

Out of respect people left a little space around him. He accepted that space; he moved in it with dignity. When he saw me see him, he raised a hand in greeting. We moved towards each other without smiling, without calling to each other as the people around us were doing.

'You've grown up,' were the first words he said to me.

'How did you know I was coming?'

He smiled an odd, triumphant smile and put his hand out to take the trolley from me.

'I've known everything,' he said. 'It's not difficult, you know, when you. . . . From the first week on, I knew everything. All about that family you were with. Everything. Here, give me that.'

I pushed his hand off the trolley. 'I'm not coming home.'

He took the trolley from me and gave me a shove towards the door.

'The car is outside.'

'Father. . . .'

'I will take no nonsense. I will hear no nonsense. The car is outside. We are noted. Laura, please have sense.' We walked in silence through the crowds.

The car was parked outside the doorway, the driver and some sort of airport official standing by it. They took the cases from the trolley and put them in the boot.

When we were settled in the back and the door was shut he put a hand out towards me. I ignored it. I turned and stared out through the window at the people pushing trolleys and carrying bags. The sun was shining. People were coming home from their holidays, pink and smiling.

'I had to do it. I couldn't just let you disappear off like that. You were only a child. Anything might have happened to you. I had to know you were all right. Keep an eye. . . .'

The driver got in and started the engine. He looked up and caught Father's eye in the mirror.

'Home,' said Father.

And we drove all the way in silence.

She is back, the running woman.

I can see her now, her feet disturbing the fallen leaves as she runs.

I am dressed today and ready for the world, and I can see her below the window and a little to the left.

It was only by chance that I glanced at that

moment out of the window. I raised my head from my book, the book that I had returned to in the hope that I would find there the energy that I had found before. And I saw her flickering skirt and the disturbance of the leaves.

'As a kind of compensation from fate, it was also in the mule-drawn trolley that Florentino Ariza met Leona Cassini, who was the true woman in his life although neither of them ever knew it. . . .'

Flickering leaves.

'. . . and they had never made love.'

The leaves that fall from time to time from the rhododendrons lie heavy and dignified on the ground, they shrivel slowly; it takes time for them to become light enough for the wind to shift them.

'. . . and they had never made love.'

I have no expectations.

I remember saying that to him.

I never knew whether he understood what I said to him.

I never knew whether he listened to what I was saying to him.

At that moment, or any other moment.

That was what he had stolen from me . . . the expectation of love, joy, peace. Perhaps most of all, peace.

I have never been able to find peace inside my head.

He never understood.

The destroyer never understands.

I put the book down on the table beside me, but there is no longer any sign of her.

The leaves stir in the wind.

Maybe it was only the wind, a luminous wind that I saw all the time.

I can hear Maurice in the kitchen working the coffee grinder.

I must go down.

I am well again.

I am glad that I have seen her again.

Glad she still runs under the trees.

Or maybe it is only, always, the wind disturbing the leaves.

'Maurice.'

'Dote.'

He looked up from the paper as she came into the kitchen.

She walked across the room and sat down opposite him.

'Coffee?' he asked.

She shook her head.

'Something to eat? You look like you'd blow away with a gust of wind. We must fatten you up. You look like a beautiful ghost.'

'What day is it?'

He indicated the pile of papers on the table.

'Sunday.'

'Oh, Lordy me! I'll have an apple.'

She took one from the bowl of fruit placed exactly in the centre of the table.

'There's not much fattening in an apple.'

'I don't want to be fat. Just well, healthy, full of beans. Have I ever been full of beans?'

He shook his head.

'Never. That's what I like about you. Full of mystery, no vulgar sparkling.'

'Really? I thought you rather liked the vulgar sparkle.'

'Don't snipe at me, dote. Everything has its place. Every man has his needs.'

'And woman perhaps, also, has needs?'

'I don't understand women. I take them as they come.'

'And go.'

He smiled. 'And go.'

'We speak in riddles.'

'Our lives are riddles.'

'If I left . . . went away . . . would you. . . .'

'No. I wouldn't countenance it, Laura. I would be bereft. I hope this is some spurious question.'

She looked at him for a long time.

His fingers marched nervously on the *Sunday Times*.

'Yes,' she said. 'It is. Quite spurious.'

He sighed.

'You had me worried. I can't imagine life without you around, dote.'

'It would probably be a lot easier for you. More fun and all that.'

'I have fun . . . but you are my treasure. Like one of the objects that you love so much, crowding this house out, one of those things that you dust and polish and cosset. They and you are treasures. Even when you get ill, I get pleasure out of looking after you. A bit crazy, I suppose. Your father said to me. . . .'

'Him . . . he. . . .'

'. . . Laura's a bit unstable. . . .'

'He said that?'

'Did I never tell you before? When I went and said I wanted to marry you. A bit unstable. You might do better for your own sake to seek elsewhere. Those were the words he used.'

'The rotten old bastard.'

'No, no, no. I think he was wanting what was best for both of us.'

'You never told me.'

'No. I thought you might be upset. He said your mother's death had. . . .'

'It's O.K. I don't want to know.'

'I loved him. He taught me all I know about business, about handling people, about how to make people listen to you. To have been his son-in-law has opened so many doors for me. Even after you . . . well, after he left this house . . . after you. . . .'

'. . . threw him out, I suppose you're trying to say.'

'I wouldn't have minded him living with us. I wouldn't have complained. You frightened me a little bit then, by your adamance. It seemed, well . . . a bit unkind. Just a bit. But I supposed you had your reasons.'

'This apple tastes of cotton wool.'

'I supposed you had your reasons.'

She put the bitten apple back in the bowl.

'Oh, yes. I had my reasons. He knew my reasons.'

Maurice leaned forward and took the apple out of the bowl.

'That's a bit disgusting,' he said.

'Yes,' she said vaguely.

She disappeared into silence. After a few moments he picked up the paper and continued to read.

'I think I'll go to church,' she said after a long time.

He didn't look up from the paper.

'Sure you're feeling well enough?'

'Oh, yes.'

'I'll drop you down. What time is your . . . ah . . . service?'

She smiled slightly. 'Eleven. Same as usual.'

He rustled the paper and didn't say a word.

'Service,' she said. 'Morning Service. Matins, if

you like. Morning Prayer, I think it is properly called. "O come let us sing unto the Lord; Let us heartily rejoice in the strength of our salvation. Let us come before his presence with thanksgiving: and show ourselves glad with him in psalms." I could speak the whole service from start to finish. That's pretty amazing, really, considering how seldom I go. It's like the marrow in my bones. Embedded. I suppose it's the same with everyone.'

'Go and get dressed or you'll be late,' was all he said.

Maurice dropped her at the church on the dot of eleven.

The sky was turbulent with clouds but the rain held off. The sound of the organ reached her as she opened the car door.

'Thanks,' she said as she got out, and her skirts whirled in the wind.

He looked at the six cars parked along the road by the gate.

'You should try ours, dote. On days like this it would be warmer.'

'I hate crowds.'

The wind bullied her across the carefully raked gravel and into the porch.

She smoothed at her hair before she entered the church.

I will arise and go to my father and will say unto him, Father. . . .

The sound of her feet on the grating seemed to drown out the words.

. . . I have sinned against heaven, and before thee. . . .

Where's the matter anyway, she thought. Doesn't each one of us here know it by heart?

. . . and am no more worthy to be called thy son.

She stepped into her pew under the brass plaque on the wall.

Lost at sea.

In loving memory.

She knelt down.

Mother, I have sinned against heaven and before thee and am no more worthy to be called thy daughter.

Was I worthy then, when I said all that to you?

I knew, because he had told me, that it would shatter all our lives if I told you, if I told anyone.

Forgive me, Mother.

I should have held my tongue.

Maybe you would still be here now, an old imperious lady with a loud voice and a walking stick. A stereotype.

I always wondered if you knew.

O forgive me, Mother, for even thinking such a thought.

Not everything, of course, but sort of turned a blind eye. Anything for a quiet life.

Would that have been in character?

Maybe you even thought that I was happy.

I must disabuse myself of such thoughts.

All I wanted was help. Safety. Reassurance. Love.

I loved you both so much.

Yes.

Forgive me, Mother.

I am your daughter.

Forgive me for saying those words.

Forgive me for doubting you.

Forgive me for killing you.

Forgive me.

But Thou, O Lord, have mercy upon us, miserable offenders. Spare Thou them, O God, which confess their faults. Restore Thou them that are penitent.

Restore.

'Mrs Quinlan?' The voice was tentative.

She looked up and found the rector standing by her.

'Oh . . . I. . . .'

'Are you all right?'

The church was empty but for the two of them.

'Oh . . . yes. I'm. . . .'

'I just thought I'd come and see if you were all right. I'm sorry to have disturbed you.'

She got to her feet and rubbed at her face.

'No. No. You haven't disturbed me in any way. How dreadful, I've missed the service. Morning Prayer. I was so preoccupied.' She gestured towards the brass plaque.

'I never knew your mother. She was before my time.'

He went a little red.

'Forgive me. That sounds a little. . . .'

He searched hopelessly for an appropriate word.

'Can I give you a lift home?'

'I'm all right, thank you. The walk will do me good.'

'It's very blowy. I gather you haven't been well. Are you sure . . . ?'

'Quite sure. I'm quite, quite sure.'

They stared cautiously at each other for a moment and then Laura put down her hand and picked up her prayer book. It had been Mother's prayer book; it had a soft, worn, leather cover and gilding on the edges of the thin pages. *Book of Common Prayer* was written on the cover in gold. That always made her smile a little, as prayer, to her anyway, was really so uncommon. She nearly said this to him, but just held the book out in a small gesture of farewell and then turned and walked up the aisle, her feet clattering as they had when she came in an hour before.

He cleared his throat, and remained standing by her pew until she had reached the door.

'Mrs Quinlan.'

She turned round.

'If I can ever be of any help. . . .'

'Thank you.'

'. . . I do hope you will call on me.'

She couldn't remember his name. It wasn't Mr Burroughs; he was dead and buried in the plot at the back of the church.

'Thank you. Rector. Yes. Thank you. I will remember that.'

The door creaked as she pushed it open.

The sun had come out and bright leaves danced across the gravel.

'Goodbye,' she called to him, and pulled the door closed before stepping fully out into the wind.

Maurice was talking on the telephone in the hall when she arrived home.

He turned as she opened the door and gave her a little flip of the hand.

'Yes,' he said into the mouthpiece. 'Yes.'

Laura walked past him towards the kitchen.

'Yes,' she heard him say. 'I'll make it up about three. All things being equal. Yes.'

She was filling the kettle when he came into the kitchen. He came over to her and put his hands on her shoulders and kissed her on the top of her head.

'I'll make coffee,' he said, taking the kettle out of her hand. 'You sit down. I'll make lunch. How are you feeling, dote? O.K.? How was church?' He plugged in the kettle and pressed the switch, opened the press above his head, and took out the coffee grinder.

'There's some smoked salmon in the pantry. Present from the O'Briens. He has this guy who smokes all his salmon for him. It's great to have friends in high places. We'll have smoked salmon and scrambled eggs. Sublime, I think. How does it suit you? Don't move, dote. I am filled with energy.'

He poured the coffee beans into the grinder.

'Should you pop up and have a sleep after lunch? Would that be a good idea? You need to take care of yourself, you know.'

He pressed the button on the grinder and the machine bellowed. He always kept his finger on it too long and Laura always tensed herself, waiting for an explosion.

'Good sermon?' he asked as soon as there was silence.

'Fine,' she lied.

'I just whipped in and out, stood at the back, like one of the lads. It was Father Mullarny, not a brain in his head. It's fellows like Mullarny bring the Church into disrepute. How many eggs?'

He stopped talking and looked at her.

'Are you O.K.? Really, truly O.K.?'

'I'm fine. Two eggs for me. I'll get the smoked salmon.'

'You'll do nothing. You're not to move a finger. Rest yourself. I am in charge. A glass of wine? Why not?'

He took a bottle from the fridge and put it on the table. He picked two glasses from the shelf and put them beside the bottle. He pulled the cork from the bottle and poured them each a glass. He lifted his glass and held it out towards her.

'Dote. To you, my dote. *Sláinte.*'

She smiled and picked up her glass.

'Who was on the telephone?'

She held her glass up in acknowledgment of his toast.

'Oh God, bloody boring. I was just going to tell you.'

He cracked eggs into a basin and flipped at them with a fork.

'You'd think they could leave you alone on a Sunday.'

He put some butter into a saucepan and watched as it melted, frowning slightly.

'Who?' she asked.

'It was the secretary to the Secretary of the Department. You remember I was off in Europe with the Minister. You remember? Just before you were. . . .'

She nodded.

'Well, now the Brits are being difficult again about subsidies . . . that sort of thing. Difficult to explain, but it's a bit dramatic at the moment and he wants to have a word with me. Now, I won't go . . . I positively won't go, dote, if you don't feel well enough. This can all wait until tomorrow. I said that to him. . . . Can't this wait until tomorrow? But you know those civil servants; if they ever move at all they want to move like lightning. We want to keep ahead of the posse, that's what he said to me.'

Laura started to laugh.

He stopped stirring the eggs.

'What's so funny?'

She shook her head and continued to laugh, helpless explosions of laughter.

The butter was foaming furiously in the saucepan. He took it off the flame.

'There are times I don't understand you,' he said.

She collected herself.

'I feel so pleased to be back in life again. I'm fine I promise you.'

He poured the eggs into the pan and stirred furiously.

'Are you absolutely certain that you'll be all right?'

'Of course I'm certain. I'll potter round, read a bit, and go to bed early.'

'That's the girl. That's my splendid girl.' He sounded relieved.

'Don't let those eggs get too hard.'

He pulled the pan off the heat.

'Grain subsidies,' he said, and left the room to go and get the smoked salmon.

The sun escaped from the clouds from time to time and threw shadows on the grass and the stubble fields and the multicolours of the turning leaves. As they turned into the hollow it was caught in the clean windows of the summerhouse and quivered there like staring golden eyes.

'What do you think?' His voice was nervous.

The wooden balcony and the door were mended, good as new, and they and the window frames were scoured and ready for painting.

'It's great,' she said at last. 'I never imagined it would be so. . . .'

'It was Maurice insisted that this man from the mill. . . .'

'. . . perfect.'

'I wanted to do it all myself, but he said. . . .'

'Shamie Doyle.'

'. . . no. He said no.'

'Shamie's a craftsman. He likes to get things just right. Perfect. He knows about perfection.'

'There wasn't much for me to do. I just came

lown each day and felt redundant. I cleared back
o the stream. That was the job I did. I do hope. . . .'

'I am so astonished. Thank you.'

'I hope it pleases you. That's what we all wanted
to. . . .'

She stepped up beside him and kissed his cold
cheek.

'Thank you.'

They began to walk slowly across the grass; it
bent under their feet, leaving a silver trail behind
them.

'It's lucky we put on the boots,' she said. 'Let's
just walk round it first. I'd like to do that. Before
. . . before. . . .'

He took her hand and they walked where the
undergrowth had been. The earth was still brown
and now covered in leaves, but next year the grass
would grow again. Willow, rhododendron, birch,
and behind them a huge chestnut, all now had their
own space. The stream, full after the rain, spread
itself between its narrow banks.

They walked in silence.

'. . . before going in.' She finished the sentence
as they approached the steps. 'I have to go in.'

'Of course you have to go in. You have to see
what a great job we've made of it.'

'Yes.'

She disentangled her fingers from his hand and
went up the steps.

He didn't know whether to follow her or wait
and see if she might call him. He stood undecided,
with one foot on the bottom step.

This time the door opened with ease. Light came
in through the windows and lay peacefully on the
bare floor.

She stepped inside.

'Laura.'

He had been sitting on the sofa and stood up as she stepped in through the door.

Surprised by his presence, she took a step back towards the evening sunlight.

'Don't go, child. Come here to me. Why are you always running away from me?'

'You know well.' Her voice trembled.

'Laura!'

Dominic's voice called to her from outside in the evening sunlight.

Save me.

He walked across the floor, across Mother's turkish rug. He moved past her and closed the door. He put his arm round her shoulders and walked her back across Mother's turkish rug, orange, blue, pink stripes under their feet, to the sofa where he had been sitting waiting for her.

'Laura!'

Please save me.

'I am your father. I would never hurt you. We must talk this through. I don't want you to hate me, Laura.'

As he spoke he pushed her down onto the sofa. He took the book from her hand and tossed it onto the floor where it lay spine up, tented on the turkish rug.

'I don't hate you. Truly, I don't, Father. I just want. . . .'

'Want, want, want.' He whispered the words, pressing her back, his hands pressing her, holding her, the weight of his body imprisoning her. His face was hot, his lips hot, tongue hot.

Hot tears from their eyes mixed on their cheeks.

'I am your father,' he screamed into her ear.

In the distance the dog barked.

'Pekoe.'

His right hand scrambled through her clothes,

ulled at her skirt. With his left hand he took her
hair. . . .

'Pekoe.' She tried to call the name.

. . . and winding it into a long, dark rope, he
pulled it round her neck. He silenced the only word
she could say. He pulled until she thought she was
going to faint. She closed her eyes and hit out at
him with her hands, and the dog barked. He jerked
ferociously into her body and beat and beat and she
beat at him with her hands and suddenly the dog
was there, scratching and whining at the door, as
if he had heard her voice calling. The hand holding
her hair relaxed and she was able to move her head,
able to see his head pressed down onto her breast.
He was going slightly bald and the crown of his
head was freckled with tiny moles.

We are now destroyed, she thought.

He groaned and pushed himself off her.

In the silence the dog whined again.

Laura stood up and pulled at her clothes. There
was blood on her skirt, there was a black painful
hole in her body. She could see nothing, only hear
the whine of the dog and the shocking sound of her
father's breathing.

'Why did you do this to me?'

His words startled her. He looked up at her. His
eyes were full of tears and cunning.

'Think of your mother.'

She walked across the room and opened the door.

'This will have to be our secret.'

The little dog looked up at her, his tail wagging.

'She will go. Leave us. For ever.'

She stood by the open door, staring out into the
evening sunshine.

'Hate you. Leave you. Punish you by going. For
ever. She might die. Just think, Laura, what might
happen.'

The dog ran across the balcony and down the steps.

'Promise me, under God.'

She stepped out onto the balcony.

Dominic thought that she was going to faint. He moved up the steps towards her.

'Laura.'

She looked down at him and her face suddenly filled with relief and joy as if she loved him.

He held his hand out towards her.

'Dominic.'

'Laura. Dear Laura.' She took his hand and pulled him quickly away across the grass.

'Promise, under God.'

She shook her head to dislodge the screaming words.

'Come away,' she said. 'Come, come, come.'

'Is it possible ever . . . ever, ever, to leave the past behind?'

She was tired, and he put his hand under her elbow as they walked up the little path to the house.

The house for once was silent. The windows, closed against the rain, reflected the dark, gathering clouds.

'It's going to rain again,' he said.

'I have tried to forget . . . well, certain things. Push them away out of my mind. I tried so hard to pretend that certain things had never happened. I didn't just draw a polite veil over that area of my memory . . . I tried surgery, excision.'

She stood in front of the kitchen door, incapable, apparently, of raising her hand to open it.

Dominic turned the handle and pushed the door open. She walked through.

'Laugh, if you want.'

She stood just inside the door and he closed out he disturbing wind.

'But when my father died . . . and I hated him, I really did hate him . . . in spite of that I got this feeling that I was alone. No one was there to protect me any longer. From death, you understand, to protect me from death.'

He switched on the light.

She nodded, acknowledging his presence and his gesture of normality.

'I am tired now of meeting the dead wherever I turn. I am tired of hearing their voices. You're a priest,' she said almost angrily. 'You should be able to help me.'

'I was never a priest. I wore those clothes under false pretences. I can listen. That's all I am capable of doing.'

He picked up the kettle from the stove and carried it to the sink.

'Go on up to your room. I'll make the tea if you insist . . . or I'll get us a drink. You're so tired. Let's go up there. I love that room. I can listen there. You've done too much today.'

'Yes, a drink. No tea. A drink would be great.'

She moved towards the door.

'Where's Maurice?' he asked.

'Maurice?' She thought for a moment and then laughed, a normal cheerful laugh. 'Maurice is making up for lost time.'

'Promise me, under God. I could hear him shouting that after me as I ran. What's God got to do with this? I thought that, as I ran.'

Dominic leaned over and filled her glass again.

She was sitting in the armchair by the fire. Her face was in darkness, but from time to time he could see the liquid flash of the flames reflected in her eyes. Her hair hung down around her, covering her shoulders and her breasts like a great, dark veil. He thought how easy it would be to twist it into a rope, to wind it around her throat, to choke her breath.

'He only shouted three times. He must have decided then to see to his own equilibrium.

'I ran. It was all I could do. It was quite sordid, really. I had to pull my clothes up. . . . I was so frightened that I'd meet someone. I was . . . fouled . . . well, sort of smeared. With blood and . . . stuff. And my head was full of sounds. His voice, his breathing. His horrible, choking breathing.

'I didn't know what to do. I don't think I even knew where I was going.

'Pekoe was happy. He ran along beside me. He was happy. Bloody, yapping little dog. I never really liked him much. Mother had him spoiled rotten. But I was glad to have him there running along beside me.

'I was wearing a green skirt and a white blouse. It was my school uniform. Yes, I must have just come home from school. It was that time in the afternoon. I used to go down to the summerhouse to read, about that time. No one could find you there and get you to do messages and things.

'I didn't expect him to be there. He hardly ever went down there. He never had time to sit around and read books, or dream, or waste time, as he would have called it. He was such a busy man. He had been elevated . . . that was my mother's word . . . to the Cabinet earlier that year. So you see, he had very little time for lounging round.

'He was starting to get a bit fat. Mother pointed that out to him, one day at lunch. This elevation is

going to your stomach . . . something like that. I
remember laughing.

'I didn't know he was going to be there.

'I don't know where Mother was. I don't remember. He must have known she wasn't going to. . . .
He wasn't worried by the dog barking.'

She stopped speaking at last and stared into the
fire.

He didn't like to say a word. He felt burdened by
what she had told him.

Red, orange, golden flickering light wrapped
them in intimacy.

'He must have known she wasn't going to be
there.' She whispered the words after a very long
silence.

She turned towards him suddenly. 'I haven't told
anyone. I have never spoken those words. I wasn't
able to speak like that to Mother. How can you tell
your mother such a story?'

She gestured with her hands. 'I really only
wanted it to disappear, as if it had never happened.
Maybe it never did happen. Mother told me I was
a liar . . . but then, she must have believed me, or
else. . . . It is horrible, Dominic, to be the author of
someone's death.'

'I know.'

'I'm sorry. I shouldn't have said that.'

'I love you,' he said, but she didn't appear to hear
him.

'I thought she would be strong. I thought she
would save me. Do you think she hated me for
what I did?'

'You did nothing.'

'I used to love him. Not then, not in those later
years, but before. I loved him. I loved the way he
touched me, held me. He was warm and she was
the other way . . . haughty somehow, alone. I loved

her too, but not in the same close way. She could cut the ground from under his feet in one short sentence. Yes, she used to do that quite a lot.'

The telephone rang somewhere outside the door.

For a moment she didn't appear to hear it and then she got up slowly and crossed the room, almost as if she wanted it to stop ringing before she got to it.

The sound of the ringing stopped and he got up and threw some wood onto the fire. It spat angry sparks into the darkness of the chimney. He poured some more wine into the empty glasses and then walked to the window. It was growing dark outside and the wind was getting up; the clouds looked like bundles of white rags that someone had thrown up into the air; blowing away to the west, darkening as they escaped from the dying fingers of the sun.

O Lamb of God, who takest away the sins of the world, hear our prayer.

The fields below the house were empty of cattle now that the summer was over.

O Lamb of God, who takest away the sins of the world, hear our prayer.

They stretched almost without colour and folded down into the hidden valley.

O Lamb of God, who takest away the sins of the world, grant us peace.

'Amen,' she said behind him.

He turned, startled to find her standing just at his shoulder.

'It was Maurice.'

She laughed.

'He's such an ass. No. He's sweet, really, and so good to me. He won't be back. The talks, he says, will go on long into the night. He'll be in the mill by nine . . . at his desk. Just in case anyone wants to know. Talks, how are you!'

'Do you mind?'

She shook her head.

'What right have I to mind? It just makes me laugh, though . . . this charade we play. Yes, darling, I say. That's all right, darling. Don't work too hard. It's a daft ritual. I suppose we think it's more polite than saying the truth.'

'Maybe he thinks you don't know.'

'He knows I know, all right. We trot up to it in conversation sometimes and then veer away.'

'You never told him about . . . your father.'

She walked away from the window and picked up her glass.

'No.'

He gestured a question with his hands.

'There was never a suitable time. Do you know, sometimes I used to forget why I hated that man so much. Hate took over from memory. Maurice was aware of the hate. He despised me for it. He thought my father was some sort of godlike creature. A man who could do no wrong. I couldn't tell him. He loved the illusion that he was made glorious somehow through his connection with my father. I also think he has that curious notion that most men have, that in some inexplicable way women are responsible for the terrible things, violent things like that, that happen to them. I . . . I. . . . Yes. I became ill with half believing.'

'Grant us peace.'

'Amen.'

'Hear our prayer.'

'Amen.'

'O Lamb of God.'

'Why do you say such words when you don't believe?'

'I don't believe in the priesthood, I don't believe in the Church, I don't believe. . . .'

'Non credo.'

He laughed.

'That's what it sounds like. I believe we can be healed. I believe in mysteries, I believe in the constant preparation for death, I believe in miracles, I believe in love. How about that?'

She took a long drink from her glass and didn't say a word.

For a long time she stood by the window and seemed to be staring out at the last flickering of the sun.

'Did you say the car was full of petrol?'

'Yes . . . I . . . .'

'Can you syphon out a gallon for me?'

'I . . .'

'You'll find a can and a tube in the garage. Will you do that? I'll meet you at the kitchen door.'

She left the room.

I ran.

Across the bottom of the field and along the lane that led to the sea.

The little dog ran beside me.

Joyful Pekoe.

My heart was bursting inside my chest and the roar of it was in my head and eyes and mouth. . . .

. . . and the roar of the sea on the stones in the little cove, where her boat was drawn safely up above the tide line; neat, ordered, ready to be rolled down the slipway into the sea.

Pebbles rattled out over the larger stones and then were dashed in onto the land again, stinging my legs as I walked into the water in my black lace-up school shoes.

I threw myself forward into the waves and the

sea punished me and scoured me. My clothes and hair were heavy with water and I knew it would be so easy to die . . . and that bloody dog barked on the shore . . . and I felt cold and my eyes were stinging with the salt and the little stones cut at my legs and arms.

I crawled out of the water onto the stones and lay there, staring up at the windy sky, and the dog licked at my face and his tongue scratched at my cheek, and I feel even now the scratching of his tongue on my cheek.

Bloody Pekoe, I said, and he wagged his tail when he heard his name.

My shoes were gone.

At some moment the sea must have sucked them off.

My arms and legs stung with innumerable tiny cuts and I was shivering.

I pushed myself up onto my feet and stood looking at the sea. I wrung the water from my hair. I was shivering; water poured from my clothes onto the stones round my feet. Pekoe wagged his tail.

I scrambled up over the stones to the lane and began to run towards home, not through any eagerness to arrive, but to try and warm my bones. The dog pranced beside me.

My fingers were dead; my wet clothes seemed to weigh a ton. As I ran up through the field I saw my father's car disappear away up the avenue and out of the gate.

My mother was standing in the hall when I opened the door. The dog rushed to greet her, jumping up and whining and clawing at her skirt with pleasure.

I shut the door behind me and stood there dripping.

'My dear Laura,' she said. 'What have you been doing? Look at the floor, child. What . . . ?'

She looked at my face. 'Have you had an accident. . . . Darling. . . .'

'I fell in the sea.' I mumbled the words.

'You what?'

'I fell in the sea. I fell . . . I tripped on the pier and. . . .'

'I have never heard anything so silly.'

'. . . fell.'

I started to cry. The tears were hot on my cold cheeks. She took a couple of steps towards me and stopped.

'You look a rare sight. You should see your. . . .'

She gave a nervous little laugh.

'Go up at once and jump into a hot bath. You'll get your death of cold. I can't think how you can have. . . . Run. . . . Scoot. Get out of those clothes as soon as possible. I'll bring you up a hot drink.'

'I thought I was going to drown.'

Suddenly alarmed she put out her hand towards me but I splashed my way past her and ran up the stairs.

When Dominic arrived at the kitchen door with the can of petrol, she was standing waiting for him. She had put on her boots and an old green anorak.

'Come on,' were the only words she spoke, and he followed her down through the wet grass to where the fold in the hill hid the stream and the summerhouse.

'It's just occurred to me,' she said suddenly, 'that there was only one thing to do.'

'Laura. . . .'

'I don't want you to speak. Not a word. I am generalissimo. I am in charge.'

It was all dark grey now; the green had lost its colour, the sun had gone and there was no moon; very soon it would be black. The stream murmured, and far away above them on the road the headlights of a car reached for a moment towards the sky and then were gone away.

'Just sprinkle that stuff round the place for me, please. Floor, walls, balcony . . . wherever you think. I hope we have enough.'

She stood at the bottom of the steps and watched him work. It was pitch dark in the little house, and stuffy. He splashed the petrol onto the floor and onto the bottom of the walls; then he came out and threw some onto the balcony.

'The door,' she called to him. 'Do keep some for the door.' He poured the remaining petrol onto the floor in front of the door and splashed some up the sides.

He came down the steps with the empty can in his hand and saluted her.

'You keep away.' She waved her hand over towards the trees. 'You stink of the stuff. You might go up too, and then we'd be in the soup.'

He backed away across the grass, never taking his eyes off her.

She took a folded newspaper from her pocket, opened it out, and then rolled it between her fingers so that it made a long tube.

She fumbled in her pocket and took out a large box of matches. It was almost dark now and he could no longer see her small movements. He heard the scrape of the match on the box and saw the tiny flicker of its flame.

She touched it to the end of the paper tube and he watched her move up onto the bottom step of the summerhouse, the paper flaring at arm's length. With a sudden movement she threw the paper towards the door. For a moment he thought the flame was going to go out as it hit the balcony floor, but after a pause there was a cracking noise and the door began to blaze.

He watched the starving flames devour the walls. Glass cracked and splinters spewed from the flaming caves that had been windows.

She was suddenly beside him; her hand was on his arm.

'We don't have to stay here and watch it. Come away. You can talk now. Recriminate, if you wish. You've been so good not to try and stop me. I do hope it doesn't damage any of the trees. I wouldn't want to do that.'

A gust of wind took a spiral of sparks high into the air and scattered them.

'Like fireworks,' said Laura, pulling him away.

They heard the crackling and the roar of the flames until they had turned the corner of the hill, and then there was silence and only the smell of smoke drifting through the air.

'I'm sorry.' She leaned on his arm, exhausted now. 'It does seem a dreadful thing to do after all your hard work, but I couldn't think of anything else. Fire and water, you know.'

'What?'

'Purges. I do hope you don't mind being a party to this . . . well . . . destruction. I just realised when Maurice rang that this was the moment to do it. I could never have done it if he'd been around. He'd really have had me locked up. I'll have to think up some sort of a tale for him. A white lie.'

'A pretty big white lie it'll have to be.'

She shook her head. 'I could take to pyromania. That first whoosh was pretty amazing, wasn't it? I was a bit scared. I rather enjoyed the feeling. Are you angry with me?'

'No. Dumbfounded. I hadn't realised that you had that sort of energy.'

The house in front of them looked normal and welcoming, lights spilling out into the darkness from the windows.

'Home,' she said. 'I could never leave this house, Dominic.'

At the kitchen door they turned and looked back down the hill. The belly of a cloud glowed pink for a moment, and then sparks blew again into the air.

That was all.

She closed the door and locked it.

'I'd no idea it was so easy to destroy something like that . . . and so exhilarating. Perhaps I should become a football hooligan. I'm starving. You will stay the night, won't you? I couldn't bear to be alone tonight. You must have a bath – you stink of petrol. We'll both have baths and then we'll have a feast. A huge feast . . . You will stay, won't you?'

'Yes,' he said. 'I'll stay.'

The fire had settled into a heap of glowing ash. The room was warm, the curtains pulled tight to keep out the thoughts of the echoing fire below the fields.

She lay against him on the sofa, her head on his shoulder, around them on the floor the debris of their feast, plates, glasses, fruit, cups, forks, an empty wine bottle, cheese; comfortable debris.

'I really should have waited for someone like you.'

She touched his face gently.

'Yes,' he agreed.

'I wanted to deprive my father of this place . . . sling him out. Maurice thought I was crazy. We can all live together in the same house, he said. It's not as if there isn't enough room. He got on so well with my father. I just said no. No, no, no, no.'

She covered her face with her hands as she spoke the words, hearing them echo inside her head.

The words echo.

No, no echoes.

Echo. No.

He held her tight against him.

After a few moments she took her hands away from her face.

'You must be crazy, Maurice said . . . I am marrying a crazy woman. He laughed. He didn't take it very seriously. My father moved into the mill manager's house. Living over the shop, he called it, and he never came through the door here until he came home to die.'

She began to cry.

'I think he was a very lonely man. Forgive me, he said when he was dying, and I said, Yes, but I didn't mean it. Down the years I have frightened myself with my own hatred. Forgive me, he said.'

She took a handkerchief out of her pocket and blew her nose. 'How many bottles of wine have we drunk?'

He laughed. 'It doesn't matter.'

'We'll feel terrible tomorrow.'

'Prehaps.'

'Why do you say "prehaps"? I've noticed you saying that before.'

'I always used to say it when I was small . . . well, up to about fifteen, really. Then my mother said one day, You'll never get to be a priest, if you go on saying *prehaps*. Only babies say *prehaps*. . . . So I taught myself to say the other thing, but I always think, *Prehaps*. *Prehaps* that's why I'm not a priest any longer; *prehaps* she was right.'

'We will never be alone together again. You realise that, don't you?'

'Laura. . . .'

She kissed him.

Her mouth tasted of salt.

She pulled her hair around them both and in that cave of blackness and silence she fell asleep, and he lay holding her, knowing that he might never hold her like this again.

My teeth were chattering. Every step I took left a trail of water, mud, and tiny, slithering stones. My hands felt as if they were made of stone; I could feel nothing, not the banister rail, not the knob on the bathroom door. I couldn't turn it with my stone fingers. She hurried up the stairs behind me, now very frightened, I think, by my state.

'I can manage.'

I spoke the words at the door of the bathroom as I struggled with the knob. I was suddenly afraid that there might be marks on my body that I didn't want her to see.

'Of course you can't manage. Let me open that door. You're in such a state, Laura. I've never seen anyone in such a state. . . . Take off those clothes.'

I took off my clothes and threw them in a heap on the floor. By the time she had turned round from fussing with the bath taps, the plug, the hot and cold water, I had wrapped myself in a big white towel and was sitting hunched on the chair by the bath. Water swirled from the taps and the air became moist and misty with the steam rising from the bath. I clutched the towel round me and hoped that she would leave me alone.

She talked nineteen to the dozen, words seeming to swirl from her mouth like the water from the taps.

I didn't hear a word she said.

I don't know the right words.

She swished the bath water up and down with her hands, testing for heat, for depth.

Even if I did know the right words I wouldn't know how to speak them.

She turned her head and smiled at me; her face was pink from the steam.

How can I speak to this woman?

She reached out and turned off first the hot tap. . . .

To my mother.

. . . and then the cold.

There was silence.

'That skirt looks ruined. . . .'

His wife.

She walked across the bathroom and bending down, gathered up the bundle of clothes.

'You might have been drowned.'

This woman. My mother. His wife.

'Then where would we have been?'

Where indeed?

'In you get, darling. You'll feel better when you're warm. I'll go and get your night things. There's no point in getting dressed again. Bed's the place for you. . . . Pop in, dear silly child. I've just been blethering.'

'I've lost my shoes.'

'What's a pair of shoes? You are safe. That's all that matters.' She left the room, holding my clothes out in front of her as if they might infect her with some disease.

I stepped cautiously into the bath.

I was embraced by the kindness of the water. I was warmed. I lay with my eyes shut, feeling the warmth taking hold of me. I lay right back so that only the island from above my eyes to the tip of my chin was above the water. I heard no sound, only the water sighing in my ears, and the steam rose round me and the words in my head were unfrozen. I opened my eyes and found her standing above me smiling down at me; glad, I'm sure, to see me normal again. And I felt a terrible sorrow for her and I wished that the words were still frozen in my head.

I sat up, and she took my hair in her hands and wrung the water from it and the water tumbled back down into the bath. She wound it into a rope and held it on top of my head, and she wrapped a towel round my head like a turban.

'Bridie's making you some cocoa. Look at your poor legs – all scraped with stones.'

She held out another towel and I stood up and stepped out of the bath and she wrapped it warmly round me and rubbed my back and arms and legs.

'Where's Daddy?'

'He's away out somewhere. He passed me on the road going like the hammers of hell. He must have been late for a meeting or something. He didn't say that he'd be out for dinner, so I don't expect he'll be too long. It's lucky he wasn't here when you came in like that. Here, put on your nightie and your dressing gown, we don't want you to get chilled again. You're still shivering.'

'I have to tell you something.'

'Into bed first. Run along. No hanging about.'

'No. I have to say something quickly.'

She was folding up the towel.

'Do what you're told, dear.'

'Daddy did something dreadful to me.'

She hung the towel neatly on the wooden towel horse and then bent to pull the plug from the bath.

'What was that, dear?' Her voice was reasonably uninterested.

'In the summerhouse. He. . . .'

She straightened up and looked at me, her face suddenly worried.

'. . . did something. . . .'

'What? What sort of thing?'

'Dreadful.'

The words I had thought of wouldn't come out of my mouth.

'The most dreadful. . . .'

'What are you talking about?'

'You know. That thing. I don't know the name for it. He did that thing to me. That's why I fell into the sea. I wanted to drown. I tried to and then I . . . couldn't. Please don't be angry. Please don't kill me.'

'I'm not sure what you're trying to say, Laura, but you're frightening me. I wish you would be more clear.'

I just shook my head.

'I can't,' I whispered.

'Of course you can.'

'I haven't the words.'

She took a step towards me and I thought for a moment that she was going to hit me.

'Don't. . . .'

I put my hands up to protect my face.

'Of course you have the words. Laura! What did he do that was so dreadful?'

'Rape.' I whispered the terrible word, and I felt myself blushing as I said it – as if I were lying, I thought, blushing as if I were lying.

'I'm not lying,' I said to her. 'I promise you I'm

ot lying.' There was just the cheerful sound of the bath water running, gurgling down through the pipes.

'Do you know what that word means?' she asked me at last.

'Yes.'

'If I thought you were telling the truth, I'd kill him,' she said.

'I am telling the truth. Why do you think I wanted to go away to boarding school?'

'You mean he's been doing this for ages?'

'Not this. Not exactly that . . . thing, but he's been. . . .' The words dried up again.

'Sometimes,' she said, 'girls invent this sort of thing. Boys do, too . . . children . . . for some purpose of their own. Sometimes that happens. Children who are, perhaps, slightly mad or perhaps vindictive. Something like that. . . .'

'I was never mad before now,' I said, and walked past her out of the bathroom.

I went into my bedroom and sat down on the bed. It had been turned neatly down, ready for me to slip inside it, and I could see the slight bulge where a hot water bottle had been put between the sheets. On the table beside the bed was a large mug of cocoa. I could see that a wrinkled skin was forming on the top. I was shaking. I had to press my hands tight together to stop the trembling.

There was nothing in my head, no past, no future, nothing; only the beating of black crow's wings.

Cracking, flaying at the hollow bone of my skull.

I heard the door open, but didn't look up.

I saw her feet, smelled her light scent beside me.

I didn't look up. Her shoes were polished grey leather with tiny straps round the back.

I tried to imagine how her face would look, but I

just saw the grey shoes – and then also black crow' wings.

I was frightened by such darkness.

'There is a fine line sometimes between truth and fantasy,' she said. 'Is there anything you want to say?'

I shook my head.

There was a long silence.

'At this moment I believe that, for whatever reason, you are telling lies. I don't want you to leave this room until I tell you to. Drink your cocoa and get into bed.'

'There's skin on it.'

'Drink it, Laura.'

'I hate skin. It makes me sick.'

'Sick!' She said the word with rage and moved towards the door.

I picked up the mug of cocoa and threw it after her.

'You bloody black crow.'

The mug lay on the carpet unbroken and the cocoa spread, brown and speckled, and the skin was ugly and she left the room without a word.

'You are crying.'

'I was asleep.'

'But you were crying. I listened to you crying and I didn't know what to do.'

'It's all right. It's someone else. It's always someone else. Some person inside me. Are we drunk? What time is it? God, I'd give my eyeteeth for a cup of tea.'

He burst out laughing and got up off the sofa pulling Maurice's dressing gown tight round him.

'You are a dreadful woman. You have no time for magic moments.'

'I haven't had too many . . . or maybe I just don't recognise them.'

'It's quarter past twelve and we're probably drunk and I'm going down to the kitchen to put the kettle on.'

'No,' she said, putting out her hand towards him. 'Not just at this moment. Sit down.'

She took his hand and kissed the fingers one by one.

'It wasn't you made me cry. If I was crying, I promise you that. I wouldn't ever want you to think that.'

He sat down beside her and she leaned against him, still holding his fingers to her mouth.

'I didn't think that, Laura.'

'I'd like to tell you right to the end. Now. I think I must do it now. Because then maybe they'll go away out of my head. Out of my life, *prehaps*.'

He smiled and put his arm round her. Warmth still came glowing towards them from the heaped ashes in the fireplace.

'Then we'll have a cup of tea,' she said.

'Yes.'

'I'm exhausted.'

'So am I. It's rough being a pyromaniac.'

'I fell asleep that night. I don't know how. I certainly didn't expect to. Young people are lucky like that; sleep seems to take them over at times. I didn't wake until she came in in her dressing gown. I think she must have been just out of the bath. She came over to my bed and bent down and kissed me. I was so relieved by that gesture. "Your father hasn't come home," she said. "There was a message last night through the mill to say he would be kept in town overnight. I haven't slept a wink."

'I thought then how lucky I had been and wished that she was also young like me and able to take advantage of sleep.

'"I would like you to get up and go to school," she said. "We have to carry on as if nothing had ever happened. I promise you it will never happen again."

'She took my hand in both of hers. My hand was warm from sleep and hers was cold as ice.

'"I promise you."

'Then she kissed me again and her face was cold and I put my arms around her to try and warm her, but she pulled away and then stood up. "Get up, like a good girl, and go to school."

'I just lay there and watched her walk towards the door, and at the door she turned back and said, "Please don't hate him, Laura. Think how frightened he must be."

'The cup was still on the floor where I had thrown it the night before. That stain never came out of the carpet.

'I never saw her again.

'I didn't know that I would never see her again, so my memory of that moment is not of her face as she said those words . . . "Please don't hate him, Laura. Think how frightened he must be." My memory is of the mug lying on the floor and the scummy stain on the carpet. That is what I see when I close my eyes. I don't know . . . if I had looked at her face . . . what I would have seen there. Would I have seen something . . . that would have made me say some words . . . that might have stopped her . . . going down to the boat?

'She must have been frightened, too. What do you think?'

He didn't answer.

'I always wondered if we could have carried on

as if nothing had happened. All of us carrying that secret, not able to speak or cry. I don't suppose so, really. He managed, of course. He went from strength to strength. He got sackfuls of letters from people all over the country after the boat was found. He had all the typists in the mill working flat out to answer them. Every one was answered. Every letter he signed himself. He wore a black tie and a little black band on his sleeve for months.

'I mustn't say any more. I mustn't sound as if I hate him. I am so tired of hating.

'You have been so kind to me.'

She put up a hand and touched his face.

'I love you,' he said.

'Yes. Thank you for that. I love you, too.'

'Then, Laura. Please, Laura. . . .'

'It wouldn't work.'

'We should try. I'll do anything . . . go any-where.'

She shook her head.

'No. Thank you, but no.'

She got up and crossed the room.

'Do you remember,' she said, 'when you came here first . . . that first day . . . I came into the room with the tea and you were looking at this?'

She picked up the glass case with the model train in it.

He nodded.

'I'd like you to have it.'

She held it out towards him.

'I know it's a daft thing to give someone who is going to set out on his travels with no baggage, but I'd like you to have it. Look! The case opens here at the back. See, there's a little latch. You can take the people in and out of the carriages. *Prehaps*, one day you'll have children. They will love it and you can tell them about. . . .'

She walked over to him and put it on his knees. 'It's yours. From now on.'

He sat looking at the gaily painted carriages, the immaculate clothes on the tiny dolls, the stovepipe hats, the crinolines, the small boy carrying a hoop. Cotton-wool smoke puffed from the chimney. The sun shone; it was an immaculate vision of the past.

'I love it. That's all I can say. I love it. I will cherish it.'

'Yes. Please do.' She shivered suddenly. 'It's getting cold.'

He put the train on the sofa and got up.

'Tea. . . . I had forgotten. . . .'

'No. I've changed my mind about tea. I'm tired.'

She clasped her hands in front of her, almost as if she were praying, and twitched her fingers together.

'Would you mind if I asked you to go?'

'Go . . . ?'

'Yes. I'd like you to go. You won't be locked out or anything like that, will you? It's quite difficult, what I'm trying to say . . . I hope you don't take it. . . .'

'I know what you're going to say.' His voice was angry. 'Go away. Never come back. Isn't that it?'

'Yes.'

'Dismissal.'

'I don't think you should look at it like that. I love you. I want to remember this evening. I want to see you forever in my mind as you are this evening. No anger, only love. You have to go. I have to stay. I would like that to happen now. Please understand me. Please help me. Please go.'

'You make it sound so easy.'

She came towards him and put her hands on his shoulders. She kissed his right cheek and then his left one and then his mouth.

'*Prehaps*,' she said, 'it won't be as bad as you think. Run along. Take the train and go and get your clothes. I'll stay here until you've gone. I'll wait in here with the door shut. I would like to say thank you for everything, and then goodbye, good luck. I hope you will find peace. I hope I will also.'

He picked up the train and walked to the door. He smiled back at her over his shoulder.

'Are you looking at me? Not the wine bottles, not the debris on the floor? At me?'

'Yes.'

He nodded abruptly.

'I love you, Laura.'

He left the room and shut the door behind him.

She didn't move. She listened, her head bent and her hands clasped as if in prayer in front of her, until at last she heard the front door bang shut and the sound of his steps on the gravel below the window.

Out of this window I see the night white and empty. Like my future – an empty page on which I will begin to write my life. I will try to embellish the emptiness of living. Perhaps I may come alive.

Prehaps.

I smile at the thought of that man, that Dominic. *Prehaps* my dreams will in the future be of him. I will see his smile. I hope he won't carry my burden, as well as the present I gave him, for too long.

The moon's light is white and hard. Nothing moves. Not even the distant sound of an animal's cry stirs the air.

Tomorrow Maurice will come home and I will explain to him how I brought down petrol and matches and set fire to the summerhouse.

I will describe the flames, smoke, sparks, crack
ing, splintering, the explosion of violence in which
the door burst into flames. He may not believe me
He may consider my story to be a manifestation o
madness, but he will not question it. I will no
mention Dominic. I will never mention Dominic
again out loud, but I will mention him in my
prayers. Or maybe his name will creep from time
to time into one of my lists.

Dominic.

Laura.

She will not run again.

The woman.

Whoever she may be.

Away.

Never away again.

Prehaps.